Heer War

Heer Waris Shah

American Punjabi Books
Traverse City Michigan
2013
muhammadbutt@charter.net
ISBN 13:9781484994221
10: 1484994221

Dedication

To my Grandchildren:
Rebecca Marie
Anna Beverly
Maria Giuseppina
Edward Fransesco
Gianluigi

Acknowledgement

I wish to thank my dear friend Ms. Ghazala Munir for
providing me a copy of the painting
Heer-Ranjha
to forms a part of the front cover.

Contents

Glossary of Names

Ranjha	Name of a tribe, also Dhidu Ranjha
Ranjhan	Ranjha, familiarly
Mouju	Mouju Chaudhary
Chaudhary	Mouju Chaudhary
Mouju Chaudhary	Chief of the Ranjha tribe, father of Dhidu
Dhidu	Dhidu Ranjha, son of Mouju Chaudhary
Sial	Name of a tribe
Heer	Heer Sial, daughter of Choochak Sial
Choochak	Choochak Sial, chief of Sial tribe, Heer's father
Mullah	Minor religious leader usually attached to a Mosque
Kadi	Judge in a religious court
Kaido	Village beggar, villain
Ludden	Ferryman
Milki	Heer's mother

Sultan	Heer's brother
Saida	Saida Khera, the man to whom Heer is married forcibly
Khera	Name of a tribe
Ajju	Ajju Khera, Saida's father, chief of the tribe Khera
Sehti	Sehti Khera. Daughter of Ajju Khera, sister of Saida Khera, Heer's sister-in-law
Jut	Yeoman
Nayi	Barber
Nyen	Barber's wife

Preface

Heer Waris Shah, an epic Punjabi poem, authored
by Sayyed Waris Shah almost three centuries ago, is
the most cherished Punjabi literary work—and
Punjabi has many great literary works. It has
remained popular among Punjabis since its first
publication. One can justifiably assert that it has
attained the status of a totem—it symbolizes the
health and vitality of Punjabi literature. This
masterpiece has remained unknown in the West
primarily because of the difficulty of its translation.
In particular, it is impossible to retain the beauty of
its poetry. I believe, however, that even the part that
can be translated deserves to be presented to non-
Punjabis.

The popularity of the appeal of *Heer* can be
attributed to the beauty of its poetry, and its ability to
evoke those Punjabi unarticulated (and un-articulate-
able) thoughts, emotions and sentiments that make
the Punjab, its culture and its people what they are.
Its most endearing quality is that it brings the Punjabi
reader in touch with the pathos, hidden under a
veneer of joviality, which lies—to some extent still
lies— at the core of Punjabi culture. The primary

source of this pathos is the plight of women, and *Heer* does not hesitate to expose this fact. I believe that even the non-Punjabi reader should enjoy a forceful and insightful portrayal of this fact.

To truly enjoy *Heer* the non-Punjabi needs to be acquainted with the nature of the Punjabi pathos. Punjabi girls used to be married off at quite an early age, which meant that their stay with their parents was very short. A girl's stay under the roof of her parents was often likened to the short stay of a wayfarer in the shade of a tree. Girls were spoken of as only passing through the home of their parents, not living there. After marriage, they often moved away to distant places, and, transportation being extremely poor, had the opportunity to visit their parents infrequently, which left them quite lonely. This was often made worse by harsh treatment at the hands of a domineering mother-in-law. Punjabis saw that women were predestined to unhappily life, but their allegiance to their tradition prevented them from making any change, so that they accepted the pathos fatalistically and stoically. They hid it under an overtly fun loving culture.

All parents love their daughters, but the relationship between Punjabi parents and their daughter was

unique. It was marked by the constant
awareness that they would soon be separated.
Consequently, considerable pathos permeated
Punjabi homes. This pathos is still present in almost
every Punjabi home, but to a much lesser extent, so
that *Heer* has potent nostalgic appeal. The non-
Punjabi reader should also enjoy the portrayal of this
pathos.

   I do not want to mislead the reader to think that the
portrayal of Punjabi pathos is the only asset of *Heer.*
Heer possesses a few other, rather unique and potent
qualities. They are:

1.   It is a heart wrenching romantic tragedy, much
Romeo and Juliet.

2.   Set within a medieval culture, it elicits the
conflict between romantic love and culture. It also
brings to the fore the conflict between culture and
religion, and the affinity between religion and
romantic love.

3.   It portrays the Punjabi culture of its time in a
vivid and insightful manner, which the non-Punjabi
reader is likely to find quite fascinating.

4.   It is more than a literary work—it also aims to
teach religion. Much of Punjabi poetry, like the *Song
of Solomon,* is romantic at the overt level, but

religious at its core. *Heer* is one such work.

5.   *Heer* is meant by the author to be a parable. It explores the relationship between the soul and the body. To ignore this fact not only obfuscates its religious message, it also robs it of much of its literary quality. For example, the hero is neither brave nor gallant, but is rather fickle and untrustworthy. This is because his character portrays the frailty of the body, while the heroine, Heer, stands for the strength and resilience of the soul. In the context of this fact the character of the hero is superbly constructed.

6.   *Heer* is rife with metaphors. If the reader does not understand the metaphors employed by Waris Shah, he or she loses much of the pleasure of reading it. I have, therefore, added "meaning" at certain places, where I explain the metaphorical meaning of the text. This part is printed in italics. It is written in free verse.

7.   Perhaps the most important feature of this story is that it contains a religious conception of how mankind should live. Likely, most non-Punjabi readers will not be able to discern this conception. Therefore, at the end I have added a poem that attempts to portray it.

In translating poetry, especially of a different culture, the problem of how literal the translation should be is unsolvable. A literal translation is unable to convey the true meaning of what is translated, whereas loyalty to the meaning deprives the story of its original flavor. By and large, I have avoided transliteration, but have retained it when it succeeds in conveying a meaning. Thus, I have kept the sentence "An apocalypse has fallen on my head," even though it sounds rather awkward in English. Other times, I have kept the literal translation, and explained it further in parenthesis. At times I move so far from literal translation, and abridge the story so much, that I end up retelling the story in my own words.

In understanding the story, it is important to understand some basic features of the eighteenth century Punjabi culture. Men and women were segregated, although most women did not wear a veil. This forced lovers to carry on their liaisons clandestinely. Almost always, if a man and a woman were discovered to be carrying on a liaison, it was assumed that they had sinned, so they were harshly condemned. *Heer* cogently depicts this deep conflict within Punjabi culture. On the one hand Punjabis

tend to be romantic and praise love loudly;
on the other hand Punjabi culture bars all contact
between men and woman, thus making romantic love
a hazardous undertaking.

Finally, the reader needs to have an understanding
of the concept of Love as utilized in *Heer*. It is a Sufi
concept. It sees heterosexual love to be based on the
paradigm of man's love for God. When a man and a
woman *truly* love in this world, they are
simultaneously engaged in true love in the
metaphysical world.

Many manuscripts of *Heer* exist, and there are
minor differences between them. I rely on the story
as told in *Heer Waris Shah,* an Urdu translation by
Professor Hamid-ullah Shah Hashmi.

I have spent considerable time and energy in
preparing this book. If the reader enjoys it, I would
be amply reimbursed.

MMB
December 12, 2013

Prologue

Heer Waris Shah has a strong religious meaning:
it explores the relationship between the soul and the
body. To understand the religious meaning of the
story, it is necessary to know some of the basic
assumptions on which it is based. The story assumes
that there are two realms of existence or being—
material and metaphysical. The two are not detached
but affect each other. It is further assumed that
"things" exist in two manners—concrete and
metaphorical. In the material world, concrete things
are real, while in the metaphysical world metaphors
are real.

The hero, Ranjha, is a metaphor for the body, while
the heroine, Heer, is a metaphor for the soul. This
does not mean that Heer is a soul and Ranjha is a
body. They are both human, and each has a body and
a soul. This means that each has a double existence.
In the course of daily life, they are ordinary human
beings, possessing a soul and a body.. But there at
times when their actions have strong metaphorical
meanings. Some of the examples are as follows.

When the tribe Ranjha settles in the mesa
of Hazara, it metaphorically means Man coming to
inhabit the earth, and start the human community. As
the story of Heer and Ranjha progresses, it
metaphorically means that the human community is
progressing. Heer and Ranjha are thwarted in their
effort to unite in love. This means that the human
beings are failing to create a loving and just
community.   Ranjha's brothers are jealous of
Ranjha, who is his father's favorite. This signifies
that the first vice to beset mankind was jealousy.
When Ranjha leaves his home and country, seeking a
better life, it means beginning of the human search
for love and justice (that is, God), which requires
leaving the comforts of home. Similarly, when Heer
is chastised and taken totaskor loving Ranjha, it
means that the human community has lost its ability
to foster love. When Heer is forcibly taken away
from Ranjha, it means that the soul and the body are
separated, which happens only when a person dies.
The human community, it is implied, is dying
spiritually. Heer appeals to her father and his love for
her to prevent her forced marriage. This signifies the
soul appealing to God.

    When Heer and Ranjha die, their souls ascend to

Heaver, where they seek each other. Since
they remained true to Love in the material world,
God allows their souls to unite, which signifies two
things. One, man unites with God; and, two, Heer and
Ranjha enter paradise. It is implies that the souls of
those who fail to love remain lonely, which is Hell.

Most monotheists should have been able to
understand the meaning of this story even with an
explanation. However, the story takes place in an
alien culture, which makes the understanding
difficult, so that an explanation is necessary.   I hope
that this explanation would help the reader to
understand and enjoy the story better.

1. Praise of Allah

Let's begin, as the faithful should, with Allah's praise
Who blessed with love the human race.
He created all; He loved all —
His Friend and Messenger above all.[1]
He so willed that love should be
The means to enrich human society,
A medium of genuine human intercourse,
And, as His gift, the primary source
Of human edification
And elevating human station.
He bestowed on love such magical power
The heart of a lover blooms like a flower.
Love is the core of a saint's identity.
It is the virtue most necessary.
If love is lost, lost is good life.
A loveless existence is vain strife.

---

[1] The Prophet Muhammad is also called the
Messenger because he brought God's message to
mankind. He also is called *Habib,* friend, to highlight
his close relationship with Him.

2. Hazara

Narrator God so willed that a tribe named Ranjha
Settled the picturesque mesa of Hazara.
Ranjhas worked hard and improved the land.
Proud they were of the works of their hand.
Women were beautiful, men were stylish.
Life they enjoyed with unrestrained relish.
The rings on women's fingers were heavily bejeweled,
The turbans that men wore were variedly colored.
Their bearing was elegant, their manners gentle;
Jealous of their honor, to their friends ever faithful.
Meaning God placed man on the earth.
With hard work man improved it,
And found a happy life.

3. The Ranjha Family

Narrator The founder of the community
                      was Mouju Chaudhary,
And still a prominent leader was he.
God had blessed him with a nice family.
Two daughters and eight strong sons had he.
He was an official of the king too.

He loved most his youngest son, Dhidu.

The father loved Dhidu; jealous were the brothers.

They wished him dead, but feared their father.

No mischief they ever dare make,

But created aspersions that stung like a snake.

They thought up accusations mean and horrible,

Distressed the young lad in every way possible.

Meaning *The first vice to afflict man was jealousy.*

Narrator God so willed that suddenly

And untimely died Mouju Chaudhary.

The brothers now showed open hostility,

Took to insulting Dhidu continually.

Brothers You eat your fill because of our generosity.

Of making a living you have no worry.

You do no work, but ogle women.

They have complained your gaze is brazen.

Narrator With sharp barbs they pricked his wounds,

Kept at him like so many hounds.

Meaning *Man soon learned the power of words*

They can soothe as well as hurt

 Narrator In time, Reverend Kadi and the Village
   Council

The matter of inheritance came to settle.

They claimed that their method was fair.

The brothers bribed them; the land was theirs.

They left Dhidu a barren tract worth nothing.

His sisters-in-law took to mean gossiping.

Meaning *the other major vice is greed*

Sister-in-law Some men are haughty,

   because they are good looking,

No good they are at sowing and plowing.

They're vain, look in the mirror often.

A life of comfort they have chosen.

No woman pays them the least attention.

Their lying and cheating is their ruination.

 All day they play music, all night sing

As if they were princes, guests of a king.

Narrator Plowing done, Dhidu Ranjha felt distraught.

In sad and deep musings he was lost.

His sister-in-law brought him his noontime meal,

Which erroneously made him feel

That the sister-in-law meant to be kindly.

He was hungry for his family's sympathy,

Which made him cry uncontrollably.

Ranjha My hands are blistered, my feet are bleeding.

The land is unfit for cultivating.

Sister-in-law You were spoiled by your father,

Who did not teach you the skills of agriculture.

Soft and lax was your upbringing.

That's the sole cause of your suffering.

Narrator   The sister-in-law's mean behavior

Made Ranjha think that his brothers were

Misled by their wives, who acted out of jealousy.

His sisters-in-law were his real enemy.

Ranjha You sisters estranged my brothers from me,

Which is the source of my present misery.

We were a rose of a loving family;

You crushed the rose mindlessly.

We were united as one body;

You led us to mutual animosity.

Sister-in-law You've had your fill of milk and rice.

The full belly is arrogant, and we pay the price.

The rumor is rife that we've fallen for you.

You are so good looking we couldn't resist you.

We are as helpless as a fly stuck to honey.

Now we have to live with this calumny.

You know very well that we could turn you out.

We have no obligation to feed a lout.

You'd have no shelter, nor any food.

That should cure you well and good.

Narrator   His anguish made Ranjha go blind.

Bitterly he condemned all womankind.

Ranjha You women are **evil;** you make toads of men.

Gross and malevolent are the spells that you spin.

Did you not a fool of Rajah Bhooj make

With show of love completely fake?

Put reins through his mouth, rode him like a horse?

No doubt there are stories much worse.

Koros and Pandos[1] in battle you betrayed

The devil's dirty game you well played.

Meaning   *It is an eternal human frailty,*

A legacy of primeval herd morality,

To extend the wrongdoer's culpability

To his group and family.

Sister-in-law You vagabond, good for nothing rascal,

Why do you like to make so much trouble?

Don't you know that if a brother-in-law is bad

His sister-in-law with shame goes mad?

All around us you've woven a tangle.

We cannot see our way very well.

It is not possible to go on living this life.

Go to the wretched Sials, you might find a wife.[1]

Ranjha   O Sister, what harm did I do you ever

That to spill my blood you are so eager?

You promised to be a sister, then turned against me;

---

[1] The two opposing Armies in the Hindu religious epic poem *Mahabharata*.

[1] Sial is a neighboring tribe. The two tribe do not get along well and have poor opinion of each other.

[1] Spitting to the side over one's shoulder was considered a very arrogant gesture.

It was nothing less than familial treachery.

Sister-in-law Eat your bread, you shame of Juts

Stop this meaningless and stupid ruckus.

Your deeds are known all over the town.

Many girls you seduced,

 brought their good names down.

Their lives you have dastardly ruined.

Their families are mad; many enemies you've earned.

Meaning *Ranjha's charm is potentially dangerous.*

Only Beauty is solely benevolent.

All its avatars are deficient.

Man is charged with the responsibility

To use his assets wisely.

Sister-in-law Cute you think your habits are.

You walk spitting over your shoulder.[1]

Your fancy turban makes you look debonair.

You show up wherever young girls gather.

If the food is not tasty enough

You throw it out in a contemptuous huff.

Work you do none, eat royally;

You are headed to your doom hastily.

Narrator Frustrated, Ranjha adopted a sarcastic

 tone.

Ranjha   I admit I started this conversation,

Because I had a foolish expectation.

It was my fault, it is true.

Forgive me my fault, I beg you.

You usurped my land, now you push me out.

That you're fair I mustn't ever doubt.

I should not have ever questioned you;

Forgive me my fault, I beg you.

That you are beautiful I do not question.

Just indeed is your every action;

I should've known you are always true.

Forgive me my fault, I beg you.

But don't be cruel to the unfortunate.

Watch **out;** ill luck might be lying in wait.

Sister-in-law   You say our girls are homely—

 you have the gall!

Then leave this place, and find a wench Sial.

Play your flute, seduce a naive lass.

You might even steal a real princess

From a far-away haunted palace.

We wish you well; we bear no malice.

Ranjha   You mock me; a Sial girl I should marry.

I'd marry someone better, just wait and see;

You would burn with mean envy.

Like a real princess my wife would be.

You deserve to be thrown in a river, for

An evil-tongued woman you really are.

Still, so that this nonsense might end

I'd grant that you have been a friend.

Sister-in-law How mean are your words! You cur!

You fight with me as if you were

My husband's jealous, second wife,

Who wishes me nothing but eternal strife.

Go and find your wonderful queen,

 And let's end this unpleasant scene.

Meaning *Ranjha's family sinned;*

Then they justified the sin.

Justifying sin is worse than sinning.

Narrator Ranjha screamed with exasperation.

Ranjha You are my nemesis, my damnation,

Stuck to me like a poisonous louse.

I leave this cursed land; you keep the house.

I leave this corrupt and blighted district.

That should end our damned conflict.

Meaning *As man grew corrupt*

He became less compassionate.

Narrator He picked up his belongings,

 but didn't touch the food—

Left the premises in a dark and sour mood.

Meaning Man sought justice.

It was an impulse irresistible.

Seeking Love, he embarked on a difficult journey.

It required leaving the safety

   of the familiar and the known.

Narrator As the soul leaves the body reluctantly,

So Ranjha left his beloved country.

Meaning The separation from the beloved

is painful,

But it is a step that must be taken.

To escape injustice and oppression

Narrator   He promised himself never to return.

He left the town and toward Jhang took a turn.

Hunger made him weak, but he was resolute.

To cheer himself he played his flute.

Narrator   People started gossiping:

First Gossiper   Dhidu left his brothers;

 something is cooking.

Second Gossiper   This is why Dhidu left Hazara.

Too hard was plowing the mesa,

For they gave him nothing but barren land.

For sure they dealt him a dirty hand.

Third Gossiper His sisters-in-law drove him to desperation.

No love he received, but plenty of rejection.

Narrator The brothers were worried about

their reputation.

They might be accused of mistreating a relation.

Alarmed, they reacted with alacrity

And caught up with the fugitive speedily.

Brothers Tell us, dear Dhidu, what's the matter?

Why do you act in this unusual manner?

We are begotten of one mother.

There should be no doubt we love each other.

Surely, your absence would be painful for us all.

Your sisters-in-law are at your beck and call.

If they offended you they did it unwittingly.

Forbear. Don't break up the precious family.

Forgive them their faults; they are human.

Is there anyone who is free of sin?

Without brothers' company living is no fun.

If you lose a brother, your arms are broken.

In this hostile world, there is no safety greater

Than when brothers look out for each other.

No friend is true, but a brother—

Brothers make you, brothers break you; there
 is no defeat bigger

Than when you're forsaken by your own brother.

Meaning *Next man learned to be a hypocrite.*

Ranjha A pauper I am; what can I do for you?

You took my land; now I leave it to you.

If you could have,

You would've

Used a noose

Or managed to kill me with another ruse.

Why do you set your mouth to sinning?

You know lying would gain you nothing.

Narrator The sisters-in-laws performed
   perfunctory gestures

To make it look that they were good sisters.

Sisters-in-law We are your handmaids; our
 eyes won't stop crying

When you look unhappy and talk of departing.

Everything we have is at your service.

Forgive us if we were ever remiss.

If you leave us our hearts would know no peace.

Change your mind; don't leave us please.

Ranjha What more do you hope to swindle out of me?

You have broken my heart maliciously.

With false talk you now flatter me.

I have no kin left; you've destroyed the family.

Your heart knows you're no sisters to me;

Of obligations of kinship you are free.

The food here is no longer kosher for me.

 I am an ugly sight: you are a beauty.

 Between us there is no bond, no tie.

4. The Mosque

Narrator   Ranjha left at the coming of the dark.

Soon he reached a newly erected mosque.

Meaning *A mosque is supposed to be the*
House of God.

But it hardly was.

Narrator He was dressed in rags and had no food

To comfort himself he played his flute.[2]

Neither the young nor the old stayed away.

They all came down to hear him play.

About the same time the Mullah arrived

 No one saw Trouble walking by his side.

Description of the Mosque:

 Built lovingly after the model of Kaaba,

The mosque was like the younger sister of Al-Aqsa.

Scholars studied philosophy and religion.

Others prayed or meditated on the One.

With the glow of faith the place was lit.

No faithless ever was allowed in it.

With copying documents many girls were busy,

 While children learned writing and calligraphy.

---

[2] The flute stands for the unspoken speech
   that touches the heart

Children came quite early in the morning.

The mullah punished them if he found lazing.

Meaning *Mosque is the womb,*

In which grows faith.

Mullah Your hair is too long, which is prohibited.

Cut your hair short; you might be accepted.

This place is not for vagabonds and tramps.

It is a mosque, not a free camp.

Ranjha   You have the beard of a pious man.

Your heart is dark like that of the Satan.

You have no compassion for a poor wayfarer.

To hide your callousness you use Shariah's cover.

Meaning *It is indeed a sad irony.*

The profane mullah guards a holy sanctuary.

Mullah   Dogs are unholy, as are beggars.

We don't allow either anywhere near.

A long mustache we hold to be unclean.

Never should it within the mosque be seen.

Ranjha *(to himself)* I am a peasant, uneducated

This mullah is worse than a peasant uninstructed.

Ranjha *(to Mullah)* Tell me, in all of life's sphere

Why is so important the one thing called prayer?

How many jewels and pearls adorn it?

What is its **asset;** what its merit?

Mullah Law breakers we condemn and

teach the law that's right.

We also teach proper ritual and rite

That carries the faithful to the Heaven's gates.

It is our rituals that the Devil most hates.

Ranjha   You expect with every breath

The smell of *halva*[1] and the news of a death.

O Mullah, you are a pupil of a demon.

Your heart has not an iota of compassion.

Mullah   O uncouth Jut, if nothing improper you do,

For you this much I will do:

Let you spend the night comfortably.

Keep your body covered properly.[i]

In the morning you must leave early.

Keep your head covered completely.

Don't argue with men of God.

Don't talk back to them; fear God's rod.

Meaning   *Like a place by plague beset,*

The mosque is haunted by the Mullah's evil spirit.

5. Ludden

Narrator   In the morning when birds began chirping

Homes came to life with sounds of curd-churning.

---

[1]   A delicacy that is served to the Mullah who
     performs the burying rituals.   the burial rituals.

The spouses who had enjoyed intimacy
Performed the required ablution properly,
And travelers measured the coming day's task.
Ranjha said goodbye to the mosque.
By and by he reached a river,
Saw a few passengers sitting there
Waiting for a ferry to carry them over.

Meaning *Man became aware that a barrier*
(river) exists in his pursuit of Love.

Ranjha (*To Ludden*) I need to get across;
 please do me a favor.
Take me on as a free passenger,
I have no money to pay the fare.
 I would be thankful to you forever.
Such a shameful step I have taken never.
With my brothers I have broken.
If I stoop to begging that is the reason.

Meaning *The body is weak*
It stoops to begging.

Ludden If you pay cash, you're my customer.
A free ride seeker I peremptorily toss over.
Cash payers I have vowed to serve well.
If you try to cheat me, I respond like the devil.
Moochers and beggars I keep at bay;
They're worse than lepers, I say.

Meaning *Ludden won't help Ranjha, because*
In reality he is his own partial avatar.
That reflects his self's baser part.
In the spiritual path there is no hurdle greater
Than the base part of self.

Narrator Tired **of** pleading with the heartless ferryman,
Ranjha moved to a spot hidden.
Played his flute and started singing
With exquisite sadness, songs heart-wrenching.

Meaning *Every man has his own flute—*
Everyone knows the speech of the heart that to the ear is
mute.
But does not always use it.

Narrator The passengers came and sat by his feet.[1]
Ludden's two wives were so indiscreet
They offered to massage Ranjha's tired feet.

Meaning *An act of love*
Even if disapproved socially
Is still an act of love.

Narrator Ludden was upset; he stomped his feet.
That didn't work, so he addressed other men.

Ludden   This conman means to seduce our women.
He is some kind of newly arrived devil

---

[1] To sit near a person's feet shows respect for that
person.

Who charms men and women equally well.

Narrator Ludden was worried, as if the Satan

Had put in his head a grave suspicion.

When Ranjha saw the ferryman so wailing,

To ease his **mind** he said he was leaving.

Soon he proceeded to wade the river.

Ludden's wives saw him and shuddered with fear.

Ludden's Wives (to each other) If you are

  lucky and find a good man [2]

Protect him like a treasure the best you can.

Meaning When you find a good religious guide…

Ludden's wives (To Ranjha) We beg you,

please don't hurry.

Your plan of wading the river is causing us worry.

The river is deep; you'd certainly drown.

Don't act impulsively; don't leave us so soon.

We'll find four shoulders to carry you across.

If you drown it would be a great loss.

Please don't leave; you can live in our heart.

If Ludden is jealous, let him smart.

Narrator Holding his arms, the women led him on,

Apologized for what their husband had done.

---

[2]Ludden's wives see something more in him
  than his physical beauty.

Brought him to a boat regally ornate.

Meaning Ludden's wives are not infatuated women:
They are angels come down from the Heaven

Narrator Ranjha marveled at his good fate.

First he in the river took a quick bath,

Then entered Heer's boat, unaware of her wrath.

Meaning The boat is Temptation incarnated.

Narrator In the boat there is a bed most beautiful.

Ranjha   Who owns this bed and its beautiful cover?

They've the best fragrance that I have known ever.

Meaning Is the bed a gift from God?

Ferrymen The boat and the bed belong to
 Mistress Heer,

Who is Chief Choochak's youngest daughter.

Of perfumes she is known to be a connoisseur.

Even the Queen Fairy defers to her.

This area is under her rule; we obey her,

For she is a beauty, but a stern ruler.

Meaning They are mistaken
The bed is a gift from God.
No human owns it.

Narrator Ludden continues to complain.

Ludden   This boat is no longer just a boat;
   it's a house of a wedding party,

Or else a place of giving charity.

The poor and the rich come and go freely,

And no one asks who they might be.

As moths gather around the flame of a candle,

So people around Ranjha assemble.

They celebrate—distribute sweets and food—

As if a saint has come to bless their

   neighborhood.

To seduce my wives no doubt is his goal;

He is a charmer, can ensnare a woman's soul.

He is such a master of wizardry

Wild birds fall in his trap willingly.

Narrator   Two sheep herdsmen started this gossip.

Like all gossipers, they cranked the story up.

Sheep Herders   This is a matter that the

  Council should discuss:

A shrewd man has overnight appeared among us.

He sits in Heer's bed, merrily singing.

His words are sweet, his speech is charming.

There's no doubt he is having jolly fun;

In bed he lies with the wives of Ludden.

Narrator   Ranjha manages to cross the river;

How he does it we do not know.

Meaning   *The river was only an illusion.*

Crossing it required spiritual intuition.

Narrator   Ranjha reaches a village, where

He is interrogated by a village elder.

Elder Dear sir, who are you; what's your mission?

How do you happen to be in this condition?

You look so frail, not very healthy.

Why have you undertaken this arduous journey?

Why have you broken with your family?

Your aged parents particularly.

Their son has disappeared; what are they going through?

   Does that even matter to you?

Meaning *The Elder is the angel*

Who examines the soul when the reach the Heaven.

Narrator   Ranjha spent the night peacefully.

In the morning he felt quite lonely.

Meaning *Ranjha experienced spiritual hunger.*

Narrator He went back to the river, joined the ferrymen.

The boat was tempting; he decided to have fun,

Played his flute, invited everyone—

The passengers as well as the merry ferrymen.[1]

This news the young Heer in no time heard:

An uncouth peasant had spoiled her bed.

6. Heer's Arrival

---

1 Ranjha, the body, is weak and succumbs to
   temptation..

Accompanied by her friends, drunk with her beauty,

An angry Heer arrived speedily.

Long strands of pearls hung from her ears.

Compared to fairies, she was prettier.

She was dressed richly; so well did her blouse fit

Those who saw her lost their wit.

The diamond on her nose, bright as a star,

Made her look even prettier.

Ferrymen Come beautiful, don't be so proud.

Your beauty is short lived like a cloud.

Others pitched their tents at this place.

Their reign, remember, was only a few days.

Narrator Everyone is experiencing a sense of dread.

This immature girl has lost her head.

The Heaven has given her plenty of beauty

What she does with it, It is waiting to see.

Meaning *Heer has inner as well as outer beauty.*

Which one would she identify with?

Narrator Heer bid the ferrymen to come;

 they came hastily.

No explanation she gave, but whipped them harshly.

Heer My boat you let a stranger enter.

Foolish people, you have roused my anger.

Ferrymen Young lady, please don't be so rash.

After all we are human, not worthless trash.

True, you are beautiful, wealthy and powerful,

Don't lose fear of God; don't be so cruel.

Heer   Since my father is the ruler here,

The insolent ones I punish without fear.

I'll drag him out, throw him on his head.

He has the gall: dares sleep in my bed!

Is he a lion or the son of a king?

That with fear I should cringe?

I will make him beg mercy.

In my book he is a nonentity.

Meaning *Heer has not loved yet, is immature.*

Heer *(To Ranjha)* Get up you lazy, sleepy head

Stretched like a carcass in my private bed.

Where did you spend a night sleepless?

Are you engaged in some shady business?

Why do you need to sleep so late?

Is it your doing, or is it your fate?

You saw the bed of a husband-less woman

And thought you'd exploit the vulnerable situation.

Is it a ghost, a witch, or a fever?

That holds you so firmly in its power?

Narrator Heer advanced, a lash in her hand;

Meaning *The soul tries to wake up the body*

From its spiritual slumber, but

does not quite know yet how to do it.

Narrator The fairy meant to be the nemesis of the man.

She looked at him, and all of a sudden

She completely forgot her intended mission.

A great miracle occurred all of a sudden:

The fairy lost her heart to the man.[1]

Ranjha said, "What's it, dear?"

Heer lost her heart then and there.

A flute under his arm, rings in his ears,

 and clothes disheveled,

He was the handsomest man she saw ever.

His charming gaze touched her heart.

She knew for certain she was caught.

Meaning *The gift of love is from God.*

It is free, not earned, but

what man does with it is his responsibility.

Heer It's a good thing I didn't strike you.

Come, sit by me; I love you.

Let's sit together and talk of love.

We'd suit each other like hand and glove.

8. Ranjha's Response

Narrator *Ranjha acts demurely.*

---

[1] Heer's readiness to love means the soul's readiness
   to love.

Ranjha   Life is a dream; we know not why
We come, we live, and soon we die.
People in your position have the duty
To help wayfarers and take care of the needy.
One should not be too proud of one's beauty,
And over a bed lose amicability.
I have put myself in God's hand.
Short is our stay in this ephemeral land.
Meaning *Ranjha acts demurely.*
The body does not feel entitled
to be loved by the soul.
Heer There is no quarrel; this bed is yours.
I am yours; everything I own is yours.
As soon I saw you I lost my heart.
Nothing can tear me from you apart.
 Meaning *The bond of true love*
No physical force can break.
Heer I didn't say a word that was bad.
Tell me, then, why are you mad?
I beg you; I'd do anything for you.
Gladly I'd renounce my family too.
You said, 'What's it, dear?' and I felt accepted.
Why do you now make me feel rejected?
I had friends, but I was lonely;
God has sent you in order to save me.

Ranjha I grant you are as beautiful as a fairy,

But you are too proud of your beauty.

Fun and games occupy you every moment.

Also, you are addicted to self-adornment.

A lover, a beggar,[1] and a black serpent

Can only be tamed by magic potent.

You beautiful girls don't see love through.

To it you are loyal as long as it suits you.

Your bed didn't lose any of its beauty.

Why did you behave so miserly?

Meaning *The body fears that the soul might*

Also be weak, like itself.

Narrator The words hurt Heer grievously;
  she was mortified.

She thought she couldn't bear it, would die.

You can kill a human without a dagger.

Words do the job infinitely better.

Heer More than anything I love you.

Now, dear, tell me something about you

To come to this land, who forced you?

---

[1] The word beggar means street beggar, but also
means an ascetic or religious person—
like a mendicant—who has renounced the
world, and lives on begging. He has the status
of a minor holy man. In *Heer,* the word is
mostly used in its latter meaning.

Did a proud beauty contemptuously spurn you?

So you roam aimlessly the world all over,

Seeking a little comfort, finding it nowhere.

Meaning *Did God* not respond to your prayer for love?

Heer Or have you abandoned someone who loves you,

And this act now you bitterly rue?

Meaning *Did you forsake God?*

Heer What is your caste; what country do you belong to?

Whoever you are I love you.

Meaning *The soul, like God, loves unconditionally.*

Heer I wish you'd do this for me: Get hired by my father.

My father would be your employer, you my master.

We have to find a way to keep in touch.

We can overcome our difficulty pretty much[1]

If you would agree with my suggestion.

There is no alternative; the problem is a hard one.

Ranjha If a beauty like you is the prize,

Herding cows, although lowly, is no great price.

Now that your beauty has bewitched me

Your every wish is an order to me.

Still, I'm afraid of this greatly—

That counting me as another victory,

---

[1] The difficulty they face is that men and women are not allowed to socialize, so they have to find a way of seeing each other.

You might decide to desert me.

Go back to your friends; live in their company.

Heer In love with you, I am your prisoner.

Even my friends would hold you dear.

These are the days of our spring.

Let's give life a colorful tinge.

God has given us a fortuitous reward.

Let's make a paradise of the cow-yard.

Evenings I'd be in my friends' company,

Daytime by your side happily.

Ranjha When you're with your friends, you'd forget me.

I would be in the yard, waiting vainly.

My world shattered, I would be distraught,

Painfully realizing to you I matter not.

If I enter your house mistakenly,

I would be kicked out unceremoniously.

If you really mean to be true,

Swear by something dear to you.

Heer My mother may die, I earnestly pray,

If from you I ever turn away.

Without you my life is not kosher.

I would never look at or touch another.

God may give me the life of a swine

If I ever accept anyone else as mine.

May God make me blind and a leper

If ever I accept as husband another.

Ranjha   The ways of love are uncommonly rough.

You might lose heart when the going gets tough.

Think it over if you mean to be true.

Love is a trial of the greatest magnitude.

Success in love takes a great miracle.

Love is the Guru, lover the disciple,

Who must always obey the master.

If you break your promise ever,

On the Day of Judgment you'd have to answer.

Meaning   Ranjha warns Heer of the dangers of
 love, but he himself is scared,
'though he doesn't admit.
The body fears it would get lost
In the soul's vast incorporeal ocean.
Fear of extinction is the greatest fear of the body.

Heer   I bet my life knowing love is a gamble.[1]

My chances of winning don't go very well.[1]

Narrator   In his heart by now Ranjha trusted her,

Decided that he should see her father.

To see Choochak he proceeded right away.

_____

[1]Heer sees love as a gamble. This means that the soul is not
sure if the body would rise to the level it is expected to. If the
body fails, the soul also fails.

Heer came along, led him all the way.

Coyly she approached her naïve father.

She was as sweet as freshly made sugar.

8. Choochak

Heer I love you more than words can tell.

Because you're the ruler, my life has gone so well.

Responsibilities and cares I have none.

My days are spent in play and fun.

I don't know how I can ever thank you,

But this much I have done for you.

I know you need a cow herdsman.

For a long time you have been looking for one.

I've seen you worried over this matter,

So I have found you a good cow herder.

Father Come dear, sit down and tell me.

Who is he, and from which country?

He looks so frail, he would easily bruise.

I don't think he'd fill a herdsman's shoes.

Heer He is intelligent, prudent and clever.

No harm would come to your cows ever,

And none under his watch would be stolen.

He'd guard them as if they were his own.

He treats them gently; cows respond to his call.

To direct them he doesn't use a stick at all.

His face shows his good character.

On his lips there's always a prayer.

Father   What is his caste? Is he a landowner?

Is his faith intact? Who is his saint protector?

Does he use good judgment, or has he a deficiency

That is the cause of his poverty?

Is he like an army man who appears one day

And is suddenly gone the very next day?

Does he ever on his word go back?

Who are his ancestors, and what does he lack?

Heer   The Chief of Hazara is his father.

He is a pure Jut and a big landowner.

His face reflects his guilelessness.

Gentle eyes show his kindliness.

His physique speaks of his lively character.

His forehead shows his generous nature.

You would find no trace of selfishness,

Nor of greed or miserliness.

In company his speech is very sensible.

As a member of the Village Council

He tracks crimes like a sleuth,

Reasons like a lawyer, readily finds truth.

Father   He claims he understands the nature of cows,

And the ways of our caste he also knows.

He is familiar with the Village Council's affairs.

Also, can reason like city lawyers.

Then why was he expelled from his community?

Why did he leave so precipitously?

Why did he desert his family?

Does he tend to foster adversity?

Is there a character flaw that's hidden?

Does he habitually use words forbidden?

Heer In the Village Council he found resolution

Of the problems that had defied solution.

Although he is young, has just begun,

When he is assigned the job of arbitration

Readily he cuts through the knot of deception—

Goes directly to the root of dissension.

Good people he treats kindly.

Bad ones he handles firmly.

Among a thousand, he is the only one

Who doesn't have enmity with any one.

Father   I agree with you; let him take care

Of the whole herd, but let him beware.

A dangerous place the cow-yard can be:

Its perils should not be taken lightly.

And he must never get lost in play

Lest he lets some of the cows slip away.

If by any chance the herd gets small

It would be an embarrassment for every Sial.

Meaning *Choochak, his business, and his home*
Represent the world of that time.

Narrator Next, Heer visited her dear mother.

Heer   People were gossiping, dear mother,

Why we didn't have a cow herder.

Fortunately, I have found one.

Now the matter is over and done.

Our cows were roaming here and there,

Not being properly looked after.

Now they have a good caretaker.

We won't have to worry 'bout this matter.

Narrator   Heer visited Ranjha at his place of work.

Heer My father sends you butter, sugar and bread.

Trust the Providence; take care of the herd.

Narrator Other cow herders mocked him openly.

Cow-herders She's taking you for a ride,
  don't you see?[1]

A bowl of milk you'd get hardly.

Heer   Ignore them. God is your provider.

Their cheap mocking has no power.

Narrator Trusting God, Ranjha entered the cow-yard.

The sun was hot; even walking was hard.

---

[1]   These cow herders stand for the faithless.

It happened to be his lucky day.

He met five saints on the way.

Saints Enjoy your food; don't lose heart.

All would be well; we have done our part.

Ranjha O blessed ones, agents of the Divine,

This I beg of **you:** please let Heer be mine.

Saints We come to bring you the good news;

The battle of love you would not lose.

We've put Heer in your lot.

Call when you need us, and worry not.

Meaning *Ranjha imagines the five saints.*

In doing so, he abuses reason.

9. Kaido the Lame

Narrator Kaido was the village beggar,

A distant relative of Heer's father;

Therefore, per custom, her uncle.

He was known for creating trouble.

Meaning *Kaido is the Devil in disguise,*

And the Devil is distantly related to man.

   Man too has potential for evil.

Heer I've been looking for you everywhere.

With vexation I am almost in tears.

Kaido the Lame follows me everywhere.

I cannot give him a slip ever.

He has an agenda, is looking for a clue

To gain proof that I am seeing you.

In the cow-yard he smelled butter.

He has figured out that I meet you there.

Narrator Heer left to fetch a pitcher of water.

Immediately appeared Kaido the beggar.

Kaido   I am famished, dying of hunger.

Please spare me a little bread and butter.

Narrator Ranjha gave him his bread and butter.

Having received what he was after,

Kaido didn't stay a moment longer.

In the blink of an eye he disappeared

As if he melted into the air.[1]

Heer came back; Ranjha told her the tale.

Heer looked faint, as if her heart might fail.

Ranjha Who is this lame beggar?

Narrator This question made Heer shudder.

Heer O dear Ranjhan, you made a mistake.

You don't know what is at stake.

You should have established his identity.

Ranjha   I didn't know he was a spy.

He must not have gone very far; it is likely

---

[1] Kaido is a symbol of an agent of the devil.

You can catch him easily.

Heer Dear Ranjhan, you made a grave error.

Kaido has been planning our disaster.

He seeks clues that he can use

To spread ugly gossip—he calls it social news.

He promotes discord; his nature is villainous.

My parents he would approach, and back-bite us.

He would recruit my sisters-in-law too.

You hardly know the damage he can do.

Narrator Heer caught up with Kaido readily.

She first tried to talk tactfully,

Then roared like an angry lioness.

Her eyes were red with feral fierceness.

She knocked off his turban, broke his necklace.

She dug her long nails into his face.

Threw him on the ground squarely.

Beat him like she was doing laundry.

Meaning *She sought to cleanse him morally.*

Narrator She nailed him to the ground, and yelled:

Heer You self-proclaimed guardian of

  the community's morals,

Give back the food if you hold life dear,

Or I'd kill you before a minute is over.

No one can stop me; I am so angry.

Upside down I'd hang you by a tree.

I'll teach you how to tangle with women.

Give back the food, or meet your perdition.

Meaning *The soul's job is made tougher*

By the bod's negligence.

Narrator   Heer snatched some food; some was spilled.

Still, Kaido was left with a little.

Eagerly he went to the Village Council.

Kaido *(before the Council)* For the sake of the
 honor of our community

I come before the Council, and say this simply.

Here, the evidence I lay on the table.

Who cooked this food for a lowly servant?

Draw the conclusion; you are all intelligent.

No one gives Choochak advice well meaning.

His daughter visits the herder every evening.

His honor is in jeopardy, yet no one warns him.

Are his friends really true to him?

Choochak   This is mean and slanderous talk.

A crow is trying to act like a hawk.

Heer is with her friends, innocently playing,

Or in the weaving-house quietly weaving.

Kaido, you are a world-class gossiper.

You disguise yourself as a beggar.

Hashish you use in the company of your ilk,

Yet claim to live on bread and milk.

You are trying to be what you are not.

You're hiding your designs, are you not?

10. Milki

Narrator To complain of Heer, many women
 came to see

Heer's respected mother, the popular Milki.

Women It's the wrong way your daughter is going.

Of shame we all aunts[3] are dying;

Our insides with pain are burning.

How long do you plan to keep us hurting?

The Kadi has ruled clearly this way:

Loose daughters should be married away.

If a daughter is alone with a herder

It is the parents who have to answer.

Heer acts as if she were a city lady.

Your servant struts around haughtily.

O Milki, we are at a loss

Why your Heer is acting so crass.

Narrator Kaido also visited Milki

To complain of her daughter.

 It was his intent to play up the matter.

---

[3] All women in the community who are of
his/her mother's age or older are that person's aunts.

Kaido   You witch, get your daughter married.

Do as God orders; in a dungeon keep her buried.

Break her limbs, give her a whipping,

Crush her face; why are you waiting?

Why do you grin after having spoiled her?

You're causing us pain, you heartless butcher.

Narrator   Milki turned beet red with anger.

She ordered her servants to go and fetch her.

Milki (*to herself*) That stiff-tailed sheep, a whore,

She has been used by her paramour;

Her reputation is ruined forever.

Narrator   In response to her mother's summon,

Heer obediently and promptly came home.

Heer   What worries you, Mother? What's the matter?

Milki   I should throw you down a deep river.

My *own* child! You've disgraced our family.

We should end the matter silently. (Kill you secretly.)

Your passion is too strong, is leading you astray.

You need a husband without any delay.

Sensible parents should not let a daughter

Leave home without an escort proper,

Or else they repent in the future—

Might even end up drowning her.

If your brother should hear what you are up to

He would think of nothing but killing you.

Your father's name is forever stained.

You defied your parents; what was gained?

Our clan is shamed. That's what we got

For spoiling you—it is our own fault.

Come, sweetie, take off your jewelry, since

It's no use keeping up this pretense. (Your reputation

  is destroyed. No man would now accept you as his bride.

There is no use trying to doll up.)

Heer When God sent you a servant it was

your lucky day.

Good cow-herders you don't find everyday.

Whatever God decreed, it inevitably happened;

Why do you wound me with barbs sharpened?

Narrator   Milki and Choochak discussed their

 situation.

Milki   This is a time of great distress.

Our friends and foes throw barbs at us.

All sides of our world have fallen apart.

We have nothing left, but an aching heart.

I can't believe Heer made such an error

And caused the whole tribe to lose honor.

I tried to give her a little advice.

Her answer to me was colder than ice.

She looked me in the face brazenly.

We should get rid of the servant rapidly.

We have had enough of him; he has forced our hand.

Either we kill Heer, or get rid of the vagabond.

Marry her off, send her away.

To solve this problem there is no other way.

Meaning *The parents are short on the supply*
  of compassion,

Which is a bigger sin than Heer's infraction.

Choochak Why didn't you strangle her when
 she was born?

Why didn't you give her poison?

Now you reap what you've sown.

Why did you not drown her in a bucket of water

Or float her down a mighty river?

Meaning *They did not follow Noah's path,*

 But it cannot be said that they feared Divine
wrath.

 They avoided sin for some other evil reasons.

Narrator When Ranjha came home after work
 one evening;

He found Choochak angrily frowning.

Choochak Leave the cows alone; go back
 to your home.

Your behavior is getting more than bothersome.

Your moral stature is too low.

You're of no use; you must go.

We didn't hire a stud for breeding,

But you are after our girls lusting.

The Quran says this very clearly:

We should be thankful; He provides freely.

Your stomach is full, but you are not thankful.

You want what God has made unlawful.

In the end you'd be asked the same question:

Is the aim of life higher or only fun?

Ranjha   God provides for the rich as well as the poor.

He would provide for me, I am sure.

I have no desire to work for you.

I leave this moment, return your cows to you.

Narrator Throwing away his cane angrily,

Ranjha left the premises immediately.

Ranjha *(musing)* I hate this country! How I wish

All the Sial cows should perish.

The cows mean nothing to me.

A young lady once enticed me.

For her sake I accepted their care.

Now for her I no longer care.

Meaning *The body is frail; it's ready to lose faith.*

Ranjha To take care of the cows I stayed up nights,

Coped with every hardship, put up with

 every slight.

Choochak withheld all my earnings.

A great business he had—akin to loan sharking:

He kept his principal, the interest kept growing;

He kept his daughter, robbed me of everything.

Meaning *Ranjha seeks something higher,*

But does not know what.

Heer *(to her mother)* Father fired the servant

  peremptorily.

Now everybody seems to be happy.

God will provide him sustenance.

He keeps faith in His benevolence.

Meaning *The soul, being stronger, retains her faith.*

Narrator With Ranjha gone, the cows refused to graze.

In vain, other herders tried different ways.

Some stood still; others ran away.

One hid itself; another in a bog drowned.

Every Sial tried, but no solution they found.

Choochak was sorry, he admitted.

For sure, he had been squarely defeated.

Meaning *The Providence punished Choochak.*

Milki *(to her husband)* Our life is a mess.

Everyone is talking poorly of us.

Ranjha served you well—never made any fuss.

You discharged him nevertheless.

You robbed him of his rights when you sent him

packing.

Beg his forgiveness, or tongues might start
  wagging.

Our good reputation it might damage.

Fear God, and remember the adage:

The sigh of the oppressed reaches the Heaven.

Choochak Let's be prudent, and seek a reconciliation.

I'll beg him to accept his old position.

We should keep him until Heer is wedded,

When he would certainly be much offended.

He would then act erratically,

Say or do things carelessly,

Which should give us a legitimate excuse

To fire him—there is nothing that we would lose.

If we use this clever ruse

We would have a servant's free use.

Narrator   Milki went out looking for Ranjha

Milki *(in the marketplace)* Does anyone know

 to where our servant has fled?

Heer needs him to paint her regal bed.

Narrator Milki found Ranjha lying on the ground

In a bed of straw, making a groaning sound.

His head was shaved thoroughly

In the style of the disciple of a yogi.

He stretched himself leisurely, then spoke thus:

Ranjha Here sits the homeless king,
   the king of the homeless;
Here come the petitioners, seeking justice.
Milki With Choochak you had a quarrel; it
   was a minor matter.
What use is it to keep nursing your anger?
Parents and children have their differences.
That's the way the order of things is.
Don't stay away; come back home.
Think of the Sial home as your own.
Heer needs you, for no one but you
Can assist her in the manner as you do.
Who would milk the cows, fix Heer's bed,
Paint the legs of the regal bed?[1]
We appreciate you tremendously;
You are now a member of our family.
Heer is sad; she is acting sour—
Hopes that you'd help her recover.
We would leave you entirely free.
You eat as you like, see Heer freely.
Ranjha *(to Heer)* Your mother wants me
   to go back with her.

---

[1]A big and ornate bed is called regal bed. It has tall
   wooden legs, ornately painted. Supposedly, Heer
   had one.

Heer I think you should humor her.

After all, she is your dear Heer's mother.

The plans of my marriage are not yet mature.

Who knows what lies in the future?

Narrator Back on his job at Milki's request,

Ranjha drove the cows to the forest,

Then took a bath, sat down, and meditated.

Heer brought him his meal; his sustenance was
    reinstated.

Soon, in his sight the five saints appeared.

Their holy aura remained unimpaired.

Ranjha bowed his head respectfully.

The saints addressed him lovingly.

Saints You have remembered God's benevolence.

You remained steadfast, didn't complain even once.

Your devotion has earned you Allah's favor.

Don't worry; enjoy milk, eat bread and butter.[1]

Meaning *Devotion is the essential element of love.*

11. Kadi

---

[1] Since the five saints are nothing more than Ranjha's
own thoughts, the emphasis that the saints place
on devotion means that Ranjha is aware of the
importance of devotion not only to Heer, but,
through Heer, to something greater.

Narrator Heer's parents invited the Kadi.

Heer sat facing them; between the parents sat he.

Kadi The advice we give you, we give lovingly.

Relations with a servant avoid conscientiously.

They're not trustworthy, nor hard working,

And are known to be proficient at cheating.

It doesn't become a Jutti[2] to go around carousing.

Good girls stay home and enjoy weaving.

Good girls always keep their gaze low.

Modesty not for a moment they let go.

Your father is the head of the community.

That puts on your shoulders a great responsibility.

You should watch out for his precious honor;

That is the conduct for a young lady proper.

A match for you your parents have found.

An honorable man, his morals are sound.

Soon the Kheras would send a delegate.

Arrangements are progressing at a satisfactory rate.

Heer Addiction cannot be willed away;

entrenched habits cannot be shed.

So I cannot help it, I must have my beloved.

Lions and tigers can't do without meat;

---

[2] Jutti is fFemale Jut

Readily they kill their prey to eat.

What nature has designed must eventuate.

What's written, man can never erase.

The affliction of love is strange; the sufferer

Would rather die than accept a cure.

I promise I will obey you in every matter,

But I cannot renounce Ranjha ever.

I prayed for love. God gave me Ranjhan;

I must keep him, whatever might happen.

Meaning *It is partly false to say, "I love."*

Love catches you.

But it is up to you to remain to love true.

Choochak *(to Milki)* I'd rip out her earrings,

gouge her eyes,

Drown her in a river; kick her 'till she dies.

Crush her head with hammer blows.

We are left with no other recourse.

Milki *(to Heer)* He lops off the head of his daughter

When a father is disgraced by a daughter.

He throws her head down the river

And feeds her body to street curs,

Or leaves her in a dungeon buried

When he fears his honor is sullied.

Meaning *They think they are not culpable*

Killing a straying daughter is honorable.

Their god is the god of false honor
Who demands the killing of their own loving daughters.

Heer Those who kill daughters,
  on the Day of Judgment,
Would be meted out the severest punishment.
They would lie crushed under the weight of their sin,
And be required to eat their daughters' flesh and skin.
I meekly say I would obey your every order.
Please don't ask me to give up Ranjha ever.

Narrator In due time arrived Sultan, Heer's brother,
And thus he addresses his honor-conscious mother.

Sultan Bring her under control—I warn you, Mother.
Keep her sequestered. If I see her leaving home
I'd make sure her end has come—I warn you, Mother.
If your authority doesn't restrain her
Have no doubt I'd kill her—I warn you Mother.
The servant should never enter this house,
Or I'd kill him like a mouse—I warn you Mother.
If this house doesn't keep her imprisoned
I would burn it down—I warn you, Mother.

Heer My dearest brother, you know I love you.
Please understand what I can and cannot do.
Once love makes its residence in a heart,
You cannot then ever tear apart
The resident from its residence—

No matter what happens, what the
circumstance.
 A gushing river cannot be reversed
Even if by holy saints it is cursed.
You must bleed, if slashed with a dagger.
Loving, dear brother, is no easy matter.
Kadi If not of your parents', have God's fear.
Don't be so stubborn, I beg you, dear.
Your father might even strangle you.
This angry act he would later rue.
He would suffer self-recrimination;
And, furthermore, fear a legal reaction.
But if I give a *fatwa*, there should be no hesitation.
*Meaning As human condition deteriorated,
God became separated from religion.*
Milki (to Heer) May you forever burn in hell.
Your eyes are defiant like those of the devil.
If you do not make a turn about
You'd end up with your eyes gouged out.
Narrator Ranjha received a message melancholy.
Message My parents and the Kadi have cornered me.
I am fighting them off, but am in great danger.
I cannot put them off very much longer.
Narrator Ranjha called upon the saints immediately.
 Right away they appeared faithfully.

Saints   Dear child, what is your difficulty?

Your plaint moves our heart tenderly.

Ranjha The crook Kadi and Heer's family

Are bearing down on her relentlessly.

I plead with you most urgently:

Please take care of this emergency.

Saints Dear son, we've told you not to worry.

This matter we have arranged already.

Get up; play your flute cheerfully.

We have missed your singing lately.

Narrator   In front of the saints he eagerly stood;

Played his flute as best as he could.

Saints   We assure you Heer is meant for you.

You earned our support, and we prayed for you.

12. Nyen

Narrator The barber's wife was called Nyen.

Because of her disposition, she was called Sweet Nyen.

Having thought it over, Ranjha made a plan,

 And went to see Sweet Nyen

Ranjah I ask of you a favor, O Nyen sweet.

We need a place where we can secretly meet.

If you don't object, I could live in your house.

I would be noiseless like a country mouse.

In your house we could have our meeting.

It should be no great burden, nor cost anything.

Narrator Heer slipped a gold coin into Nyen's hand.

Nyen said with her eyes, it was a pact grand.

Heer Please keep it a secret; secrecy is a must.

If it's not kept secret, our plan would bust.

Narrator Next to cow-yard Nyen's house was located,

Which made the arrangement quite well suited.

So too, it was quite convenient

That Nyen's husband was often absent.

Like a son-in-law, Ranjha was catered to;

Nyen brought out her quilts—her best ones too.

She made a pretty bed, on it sprinkled rose petals;

It looked as if it was meant for immortals.

All night they gave themselves to abandonment.

Meaning True lovers find

Happiness and perfection in physical and spiritual

abandonment.

Narrator   The cows stood still, demanded no attention.

Heer went home when dawn arrived,

And Ranjha, looking innocent, so contrived

As if he had come from the cow-yard just then

To borrow some rice from Sweet Nyen.

Narrator By midday Ranjha arrived; so did Heer.

His cows followed him; her friends accompanied Heer.

Ranjha played his flute; the ambiance was
enchanting.
Heer complemented him with her melodious singing.
She hugged him sometimes, sometimes stroked his face;
Other times she invited him to a race.
She said, "It's mine," and took her turn to caper.[1]
He chased her, and she dived deep underwater.
Heer was a she-fish enticing a he-fish.
In her little net she caught Hazara's big fish.
Meaning *True joy lies in making the beloved happy.*
(The Sufi is happy if he pleases God.)
Narrator Kaido, in the service of evil ever diligent,
Manages to learn of the lovers' arrangement.

13. Kaido Chastises Milki

Kaido Your daughter is behaving shamelessly.
Her conduct is disgracing our community.
You tell me that you are helpless.
And the Kadi has had no success.
Heer acts is if she could not care less.

---

[1] Heer and Ranjha play a game that pre-adolescent
girls play. It suggests their play is innocent.

You have punished her, pulled her hair.

She hurt you all the more with her dare.

Upside down you hung her by a tree.

Threats were of no avail, nor any entreaty.

Well, then, what are you going to do?

Is it not clear what you should do?

Milki *(ordering her servants)* Bring Heer home,

 and be quick about it.

She left quite early and hasn't returned yet.

Narrator The servants went looking

And found Heer with her friends playing.

Servants *(to Heer)* O Child,[2] look what you've done!

Don't you know how worried is everyone?

You mother is irate, your father ready to kill you.

Ranjha is in trouble, for they are after him too.

The Sials have him cornered, 'though he thinks

 he is clever.

They have vowed he won't live much longer.

Like a parrot, he is happy in a mango tree—

Unaware hiding close by a hunter might be.

---

[2] So great is the respect for age that older persons of a
    lower caste talk to a younger persona of higher castes
   asif the latter were a child. The younger person of a
   higher caste, in return, addresses the older person of a
   lower caste as *you* not as *thou.*

The Sial ovens have no fire;[3] the community is
sad.

They say enough of Ranjha they've had.

Milki (to Heer) Come here, you monster—

You promiscuous bitch, shameless bounder.

You spoiled brat, your deeds are black.

You are viler that the vilest Uzbek.[4]

You venomous whore, you deserve to be poisoned.

You've pushed us to the limit; we are ruined.

I warn you for the last time, mend your ways.

Remember disobedience to parents never pays.

You are constantly fighting with us.

Mend your ways, you passion-ridden cur.

Tonight I should throw you in a river.

You evil daughter, your end is near.

Heer (To Mother) The servant stays in the yard;
 our cows he tends.

I stay in the garden, playing with my friends.

Milki You were the victim of a slander.

Fate stained the name of our good daughter.

But you were wrong when you misled us

---

[3] It was a custom that in times of sadness, no fire was
lighted and no one cooked any food.

[4] The memory of Genghis Khan and his followers
was still alive among Muslims.

And did not think of what it did to us.

Heer Stop your shameful threats, Mother.

Greatly sinful is the killing of daughters.

So if you at all fear the Hell,

Don't give me these threats futile.

Why do you keep adding to my suffering

When already I don't wish to go on living?

May God smite me with a malady fatal.

You don't have to kill me, God would be merciful.

Narrator Kaido continues his malicious campaign.

He does it maliciously, nothing he gains.

Kaido *(in marketplace)* Good people, listen to
  what I have to say.

No advice is better than what I bring today.

The Sials are dupes; they do not know

Ranjha charmed their cows, misled them also.

Soon he'd create a poisonous mischief.

Unfortunately, they don't see the hidden thief.

So beguiling is Ranjha's cleverness

He has made everyone forget

This affair might lead to a violent bloody mess.

When another girl elopes with a servant,

They'd be sorry that they were negligent.

Their women are loose, are getting worse.

They forget loose morals are a curse.

Meaning   *Women's laxity is not the curse.*
The laxity is the result of a curse.
This curse is created by their idol:
Their worship of the worldly honor.

Narrator   Heer's friends came to visit her,
To apprise her of Kaido's ugly behavior.

Friends *(to Heer)* Kaido is saying a horrible
 thing;
 Like the Satan, his little drum he is beating.
If you don't punish him, you're not worthy
  of your name.
You must upend him; put him to shame.
Teach him the lesson that in the long run
You reap what you sow, answer for what
   you've done.

Heer *(to her friends)* Lock him up in a dark
      storeroom.
Beat him soundly with a heavy broom.
Put around his neck a really tight noose.
Knock his face 'till his teeth are loose.
Tie up his legs, and throw him in a deep pit.
Set fire to his house; destroy everything in it.

Meaning *Heer prescribes punishment*
   metaphorically speaking.

Narrator Her friends and Heer made this plan:

One girl stood in each street, watching
  everything that went on.
When Kaido came, Heer learned immediately.
Carrying sticks, they all headed for a melee.
They held and thrashed him as if he were a donkey,
Threw him on the ground, violently kicking.
Like the sound of thatching was the sound of
 their thrashing.
They threw away his cap, put his scarf around
  his neck;
Tore off his clothes, and strangled his neck.
Narrator Kaido fought back, screamed and
  yelled.
Her friends kept Heer protected very well.
Meaning *In essence, Heer's friends are her parents,*
Because they take care of her and protect her.
Narrator They beat him to a pulp, then
  hastily turned around,
Using dry straw they burned his hut to the ground.
Broke his pots and threw away his pans.
Drove away his dog, shooed away his hens.
This job done, to their homes they went,
Looking like good daughters completely innocent.
In this way Kaido was squarely beaten
And Heer received congratulations.

Meaning *The punishment is also metaphorical.*

Narrator Kaido appeared before the Village Council,

Presented his complaint in a voice quite emotional.

Kaido Please see how I am bleeding all over.

It's your job to look into this matter.

You should not mind if I come protesting;

O councilmen, please show some understanding.

I could take the matter to the king;

Don't think I am only bluffing.

I could get your charter revoked.

I almost died, yet I refuse to be provoked;

I am willing to be reasonable,

Accept the Kadi as the arbitrator

So the matter is put to rest, and we can all

   breathe easier.

Choochak Go, get lost, you blighted crippled cur.

It is your avocation to promote rancor.

You are the head of the local clique of robbers,

But you pretend to be a holy beggar.

You rob the weak, exploit the naïve.

Like a hyena your life you live.

You are the one who started the mischief.

Don't come crying to us for relief.

Kaido Your girls know no restraint; they

   beat me into a string;

Burned down my cottage, broke up everything.

My bed and quilts they set on fire,

Looted my cache of hashish entire.

Like an army they razed everything.

Fairness and justice I come seeking.

Sials   You mix truth and untruth,

  create gossip malicious;

This is one of your ruses of harming us.

You promote discord between sons and fathers.

Break up relations between mothers and daughters.

Out of malice you set one against another.

Stop carping and causing so much bother.

Kaido   For fear of God, O councilmen,

Listen to the complaint of the aggrieved one.

The crime was perpetrated in a civilized place,

 Yet here I see not a single face

Showing any sympathy for my cause,

Nor any understanding of my loss.

The sacred bowl was a gift from my *mentor*.

It's loss is a loss beyond measure.

The roots of my existence they pulled out.

I was abused, while passersby looked about.

I was dragged like an animal's carcass,

Thrashed with a club like a stubborn old ass.

All my hands and knees are broken.

Please give me some satisfaction.

Narrator The council summoned the girls

 for questioning.

The girls complied after much quibbling.

Sials *(to the girls)* Why did you abuse the

 beggar Kaido?

Who was at fault; who started the row?

The poor guy moans, looks miserable;

What did you do to him that was so terrible?

What was it that the poor devil did

For which he was so harshly punished?

You burned down his abode, destroyed what he had.

Is it not understandable that he is mad?

Narrator   The girls acted as if they were perplexed;

After some thought, this they said:

Girls   He is not shy of acting unseemly—

Pinches our breasts, rubs our cheeks forcibly,

Bends down behind us, sniffs our panties,

Then tells us he has wild fantasies.

Pretends we are cows, he an aroused bull.

Tries to ride us, grunting something terrible.

Pisses in our presence, not minding the offense.

Lowers his pants, says his passion is intense.

Sials He says you beat him, broke his arms and legs,

Burned down his house, dragged him by his legs,

Kicked him hard, pulled his hair,

Destroyed all his possessions—whatever

few were there.

Girls Who invited this dog to our good community

Gave him the status so that he has immunity?

You can't kick him out, nor can he be condemned.

We did our part; you're not holding your end.

You fraternize with the trash of society,

Which encourages this bane of the community.

So bad is the situation, your modest daughters
   you summon;

They stand in the same dock as criminals common.

He is a vile man, while we are chaste daughters.

Whom should you trust, the former or the latter?

Kaido *(musing)* So, this is how it is,

From the parents of the guilty, I should expect
 no justice.

With Sials I have never had strong ties.

That's where the truth of the matter lies.

I am appalled how little they see.

Is it their prejudice or plain stupidity?

A parrot ruins the tree; they set a trap for a crow.

How ignorant they are they don't really know.

Meaning *The Sials do not know that they*
(like everyone) are on trial also.

Narrator The Sials tried to appease Kaido.

Sials   We beg you, please be patient.

The way they treated you was not very decent.

Yes, you suffered; they were unfair.

We will atone, pay back what's fair.

Narrator   They chastised their daughters,

  but unconvincingly,

Which did not deceive Kaido even slightly.

Choochak With my own eyes the evidence I must see:

Ranjha and Heer together compromisingly.

My servant I'd dispatch to hell.

We have no room for foreigners evil.

I'd lop off his head who threatens my honor.

I am a Sial, not an armless warrior.

Kaido   I will catch them together yet,

But if you still do not act

It would prove you are a hypocrite.

I'd avenge myself, don't you forget.

Kaido (to himself) I should make a plan

To catch them in the cow-yard as soon as I can.

On my say so, no one would hurt his daughter.

No one avenges a mere sheep's slaughter.

Narrator   True to his nature, he worked doggedly

Until he found a place to hide and spy.

Kaido sat hidden; all eyes and ears was he.

Like a well-trained dog, he waited patiently.

He saw Heer and her friends arriving,

And sat quietly until they were done playing.

After they had had a day's worth of fun

Ranjha's and Heer's friends left one by one.

Holding each other they lay down together.

The cows sat by the riverbank; they were no bother.

Kaido was elated to see them in this position.

The lame legs miraculously gained acceleration.

Kaido *(to the Council)* Come and see what
  wonders are taking place;

We can then talk face to face.

Choochak *(to himself)* This shameless fool
  needs to be halted.

It's high time I got started.

Narrator   He got on his horse; his sword shone
  like lightening.

Loud was the sound of his steed's galloping.

Heer heard the sound; in panic she screamed:

Heer   Wake up Ranjhan, my father is coming!

Narrator She put on an act, started crying
  and wailing.

Heer My friends played a stupid prank—
  alone they left me

I was scared; luckily, the servant came by.

Choochak The ways of God are inscrutable.

Un-chaperoned mix of young boys and young girls!

Narrator Heer proceeded toward her home,

   kept her poise well,

As if she had done nothing unusual.

Choochak Walk, daughter, walk.

   Walk while you can,

To break your legs is in my plan.

Heer *(To her father)* Poor servant worked all day;

   by evening he was starving.

No one cared how he was faring.

I brought him some grub. I see that you don't like it;

I give you my word, again I won't do it.

Narrator Choochak was so angry he could

   not think straight;

The only thought he had was to find Heer a mate.

14. Ranjha's Brothers

Narrator Ranjha's brothers this news heard:

Dhidu was a herdsman, in charge of a large herd.

They lost no time in sending Choochak a letter.

Letter We are of the same caste;

   we understand each other

But we can't figure out the ways of the Creator.

The son of the noble Mouju is now a cow-herder!

Please send him back; he left in a fit of anger.

By now to return home he must be eager.

We have not forgotten him; he is in our memory.

His sisters-in-law love him; they miss him sorely.

By stooping to herding he cut off our nose.

(Disgraced us.)

You should be warned, for who knows?

He might sell your cows, and disappear.

It won't be our fault, please remember.

Please send him back, and earn our appreciation,

Or we'd come as a *mela*—an unsatisfactory situation.[1]

Choochak's Reply   He is Heer's servant and Heer is
  young and stubborn.

She does what she likes, doesn't always listen.

Ranjha too—I cannot tell him what to do.

You tell him to come home; it's between you two.

Why did you expel this handsome man?

Does he not work hard like a man?

When dressed he looks quite debonair.

---

[1] *Mela* is a delegation that goes to another community to
    carry on negotiations. Sending a *mela* warns the other party
    that the matter is a grave one, and if negotiations are not
    concluded satisfactorily, the consequences would be grave.

What was his conflict with his brothers?

Narrator Heer wrote to Ranjha's sisters-in-law:

Heer's Letter Who gives back the God-sent treasure?

We certainly have no inclination

To send Ranjha to you as a goodwill token.

As long as I breathe I cannot desert him;

I believe God has joined me to him.

I appreciate your letter, but messages and letters

Don't recuperate what you've lost to others.

If he wishes to visit his family

No one stops him; he is free.

Sisters-in-law *(write back)* A handsome lad

you have stolen.

Where did you learn to lure young men?

Ranjhan left us to show his anger.

We are sure he is angry no longer.

Return our gem; think of it as charity,

Which we would appreciate most sincerely.

Find someone older to be your consort.

Ranjha is too young for the matters of the heart.

Narrator As soon as Heer read the letter

She understood something of the matter.

The letter suggested love and affection.

Indeed, it was an open invitation

For Ranjha to return and live with them.

Why did Ranjha not like them?

To this question Heer wanted an answer.

She went to Ranjha, showed him the letter.

Ranjha My brothers and their wives saw it fit

To deprive me of the land that I had inherited.

They drove me out of my home and country.

No guilt they felt, so their job was easy.

My sisters-in-law made false accusations.

Of speaking untruth they had no hesitation.

The husbands and wives together mocked me.

In truth they treated me quite shabbily.

'Go, find a Sial wife.' They mocked me.

They aimed to push me out of my country.

Now they want me to return—I know their deeds.

They need an extra hand to take care of their fields.

Sisters-in-law *(write back)* You write as if you are overly
   proud of your beauty.

Let's tell you, Miss Sial Snooty:

Our beauty is also thought of highly.

Don't ride your high horse so readily.

God knows our love for Ranjhan is sincere.

That is the reason we want him here.

We are his handmaids, will gladly serve him:

For better or worse we're crazy after him.

Since he left us, we've been doleful.

Swap him for a servant; we would be grateful.

Heer *(writes back)* How are you?

I am fine, wishing you are too.

I understand these are the salutations

 if you write a letter.

As to Ranjhan, it is a different matter,

For it concerns my self-respect.

I have sworn fidelity; my word I cannot retract.

But why do you want him back? It makes no sense.

You know we are in love; why do you take offense?

All day he herds cows, then returns to the cow-yard.

There is no denying his life is very hard.

He puts up with it for my sake.

I cannot leave him, don't you understand, for God' sake!

You sisters-in-law failed in your design,

But wish to continue to hold the line.

You called him names, as if he were a duffer.

Your accusations were truly impossible to suffer.

They dried him up, as hot weather does a coffin.

You're outside his life; why do you want to come in?

Sisters-in-law *(write back)* He was our treasure;

  now he is in your keeping.

Works of God are beyond human understanding.

Did you give him birth, or took the pain to raise him?

Do his kin have no claim over him?

You are like a loan shark, guiltlessly avaricious,

Complacently sitting on an ill gotten treasure.

You're making a mistake, but refuse to see,

Like the mouse that jumps with glee

When it finds in the pantry

A piece of poisoned cheese for free.

Heer Why do you think my gain is your loss?

I love him so much; for him I'd accept the cross.

His sisters-in-law refused to be his kin.

His brothers turned him b a new life he had to begin.

They didn't know what they were losing:

The biggest pearl on their golden string.

The Sial name is tainted; it cannot be washed clean.

A sword never regains it, once it has lost its sheen.

People say I'm infatuated with Ranjha's looks.

They see only the cover, not the text of the book.

15. Heer's Engagement

Narrator Choochak invited his brothers, and said:

Choochak We need to get past this hurdle—

Heer has brought us notoriety.

The simplest solution is this: We should let her marry

The servant, which can be arranged hastily.

It should solve a part of the difficulty:

No longer would she be accused of living in
sin.

This is the best we can do, for there is no
  way that we can win.

Brothers We give you frank advice on this matter.

Have we sought kinship with the Ranjhas ever?

Ever given them a single Sial daughter?

Why should we now our course alter?

How can we give to a servant downtrodden

A daughter by a proud Sial begotten?

Seek a match with a Khera;[1] this is our suggestion.

This has been the wisdom of our tradition:

Among good relations seek more relations.

Why should we now this wisdom shun?

Narrator Kheras sent a *nayi*;[1] an important
message he brought.

He begged a favor: Heer's hand he sought.

Honorable Juts followed, sat by the door;

Humble was their mien—they sat on the floor.[2]

---

[1]   Khera is another tribe that is on better terms with
the Sials.

2. A nayi is a barber. Barbers perform other
functions besides barbering, such as carrying
marriage proposals

[2]   It was a custom that when a man sought the

Kheras O generous Sials, we seek charity:

The hand of your daughter—we hope you'd agree.

If you assent, it would be a great honor.

Greatly we value your chaste daughter.

Narrator Choochak and his brothers assented readily.

They claimed they had put aside all considerations

 monetary.

Choochak and Brothers Riches are fickle;

 they are lost any moment.

You own arms you can't always depend on.

A crumbling rock your pride stands on.

Meaning *This is double hypocrisy for certain:*

Their pride is false, and false is its renunciation.

Narrator Choochak sent out invitations promptly—

Invited all the landowners to the ceremony.

Young girls received gifts of sugar and money.

Older girls clothes, perfume, and jewelry.

To join the merriment everyone was eager.

They brought cash gifts, and bowlfuls of sugar.

When Kheras received the news felicitous

They jumped and danced, so great was their happiness.

---

hand of a woman of a different tribe, he had to act
humbly and admit that he did not deserve the
woman. His tribe also had to do so. This included
sitting in the floor in the manner of a fakir.

Kheras We found in-laws suitable,

Blessed with wealth, and honorable.

Narrator Heer knew nothing of her own engagement.

They told her it was another occasion for merriment.

Now her anger was like hell's firmament.

Heer *(to her mother)* You've strung me to a

  Khera against my wish.

Deliberately you have caused me anguish.

When did I ask you for a husband? Tell me

What spite did you have against me?

And why did you hide the truth from me?

Such things should not be done surreptitiously.

You've given a fairy to an animal.

What you have done is grossly sinful.

Heer *(to Ranjha)* O Ranjhan, the situation is

  most terrible.

Let's go somewhere more suitable.

A place where we can live and love freely,

Where Kaidos and Kadis are reined in tightly.

Once they take me, there would be no coming back.

I would be stuck in the rut of a cruel track.

We find ourselves in love's battlefield.

As warriors of love, we must not yield.

To the code of love we must be faithful.

Let's be brave, fight out this battle.

Ranjha   Love shouldn't stoop to stealth.

The gossip will spread that we are shameless.

Many stories of infidelity we have heard.

You tricked me so that your cows now I herd.

Such is the nature of the species of women.

This fact is well known among all men.

Meaning *The body misuses reason*
In order to hide his own cowardliness.

Narrator All the merriment and celebration

Put Heer's friends in a sad condition.

Together to visit Ranjha they went.

Their action no doubt was sincerely meant.

Friends *(to Ranjha)*   Preparations are complete
  of your Heer's wedding.

O dear Ranjhan, how are you coping?

For years you herded cows day and night.

What the Sials did is by no means right.

On the name of the Sials it is a blight.

How it hurts us to see your plight!

Ranjha *(to friends)* O dear friends, you don't
  know the story.

Only Heer knows how she treated me.

(as if addressing Heer) O Heer, a great wrong
  you perpetrated:

Razed the dream palace that we had erected.

Chose to be married, ruined everything
That we had begun in our love's spring.
If you didn't intend to see our love through
Why did you such hard work make me do?
To the top of the world you led me,
Then pulled the rug from under me.
The Kheras are celebrating; you are looking pretty.
You've forgotten the oath of fidelity.
You led me by my arm, then walked away casually.
You started cavalierly, broke off cavalierly,
Leaving me despondent and lonely.
This is how you molded my destiny.

Narrator *After the friends left*
  Ranjha deliberated..

Ranjha *(deliberating)*   It does no good to
expose my pain.
Hidden in my heart it must remain.
My days are like the Last Day,
When the sky would be torn asunder.[1]
(I am going through hell.)
For me the apocalypse is already here,

---

[1] "When the sky will be torn asunder" is a Quranic
description of the day of judgment.

When the earth changes[2] and the world is at its
end.

The rent in the sky no one would mend,

So my world is at its end.

The rent in my heart no one can mend.

My luck has turned my world upside down.

Wailing is futile; I must not even frown.

Narrator   Next, the friends went to see Heer.

Friends *(to Heer)* We feel distraught, something
 cruel we must say:

Why did you treat Ranjhan in such a shabby way?

 How could you do what you did?

Truly, we think it looks sordid.

If you didn't wish to love loyally

Why did you hurt him so grievously?

We must tell you that you were **cowardly.**

Our hearts bleed over your perfidy.

Alas! For what did you abase your soul?

Is your body more precious than your soul?

In any case, there poor Ranjhan goes

To live in that land where wild grass grows.

His cane and flute he has thrown away.

He is going into exile, in the wild to stay.

___

[2] "This earth will change into another earth" is a Quranic
 description of the day of judgment

Heer *(to friends)* Disguise him as a girl; sneak
  him in to see me.

Handle this venture delicately.

Face to face then we can talk—you judge us impartially.

What the truth is you would then see.

I kept urging, 'Let's get away, we're losing time fast.'

He did not heed me; the opportunity is lost.

Narrator That night the girls sneaked Ranjha in.

Heer   *Bismilla,*[1] your visit is a precious gift.

 Please come in.[2]

Ranjha   It is no secret; all the folks know.

Heer is getting married with great pomp and show.

People come in throngs to see the merry occasion.

I too have come to witness the celebration.

You've chosen to be a bride; your love you've sold.

 What hope do I have when the Kheras have the gold?

Narrator Ranjha did not stay to hear Heer's reply.

Afraid of the truth, he stuck to his lie.

Narrator   The Kheras engaged a Brahman to
find an auspicious date.[1]

---

[1] Muslims often say *bismilla* (I begin in the name of
God) at the start of an activity. To say *bismilla* when a
guest arrives shows the host's eagerness to welcome
the guest.

[2] These are also commonly used words of welcome.

[1] A brahman is a Hindu religious leader, who performs

It was the ninth day of *Sawan,* at night, late.
The Sials busied themselves with the wedding
 preparations.
The Kheras too got ready for the coming celebrations.
Ranjha May God send a demon fierce and potent
To haunt every guest and wedding participant.

16. Wedding Celebrations

Narrator Rice and meat, lentils and yogurt
Were freely distributed among the poor—
Pot makers and milk carriers,
And servants, barbers, and horse riders.
The travelers who happened to pass through
Were cordially invited too.
Ranjha (*musing*) The strong usurp what belongs
 to the weak;
The weak live in fear, don't make a peep.
They spread their bitterness passively:
At times they wish to kill, sometimes want to die.
Unable to decide, they remain paralyzed.

---

divinations and religious rites. This includes divining
 auspicious time for an important event. Many of the
 Hindus who converted to Islam continued to employ
 brahmans.

The weak are readily blamed, the powerful
never.
 The strong share their spoils with each other.
The weak have only their sorrows to share.

Meaning *The body implies he is destined to be weak;*
    That his weakness is not his fault.

Narrator To carry the rice, Choochak employed
  water carriers.
Fragrant saffron they brought, and rice of
 different colors.
From Kabul came pearl rice, the staple of fairies.
From Kashmir white rice in large quantities.
The females were pretty; even fairies were jealous.
As beautiful as Pudmony,[1] their perfumes delicious.
 No catastrophe struck; there was no apocalypse.
Heer got married; the Heaven remained tight-lipped.
Heer and Ranjha had no clue
Of the trial they were going through.

In inviting , Choochak was generous.
Twelve casts he invited, and five groups of
 higher status.
Some wore silk shawls, some Chenabi skirts.

---

  1   A legendary beautiful woman.

Young girls mocked the groom, made fun of his
cohorts.[2]

Others sang *Sehra*[3] in a sweet and melodious tune.

Many other sweet voices joined them pretty soon.

They looked begotten of fairies, their bearing
   handsome.

Some let their shawls drop, exposing their bosoms.

One looked coyly in her hand-held mirror.

Yearning dandies now yearned even more.

Like a vendor exposes his wares,

So the young girls bared theirs.

Some clapped, danced and sang *ghori.*[2]

Like a cuckoo others sang sweetly.

 A number of artists led the wedding party,

Most of them of the caste *Marassi.*[3]

---

[2] It is a custom that the young girls from the bride's
   clan sing songs that belittle the groom in jest, telling
   him that he does not deserve the bride   whom he has
   come to claim.

[3] *Sehra* is the hat strung with flowers that the groom
   wears. The song that praises *Sehra* is also called
   sehra.

[2] *Ghori* means mare. *Ghori* is a song that praises the
   mare that the groom rides.

[3] *Marassis* were the entertainer caste. They were
   highly regarded, and often performed at the courts
   of kings, sultans, and rajahs. Anthropologists
   maintain that a Sultan sent some of them as a gift

Many singers displayed their skill

While the musicians gave the guests their fill.

They played quite a few instruments.

There was no shortage of entertainment.

The Kheras had sent invitation to all.

Young men arrived, handsome all.

They had sprinkled gold dust on their turbans.

Their horses also wore golden ornaments.

Some carried lances, some had been drinking.

Flowers from their turbans were stylishly hanging.

Next they distributed copper coins among the poor.

The poor appreciated the little treasure.

Next came the fireworks; sprinklers spewed fire.

The elephants and peacocks wore bright attire.

The firecrackers went pop, pop, pop.

The stars came down like monsoon drops.

The fire-mice scurried about mischievously.

The wheat grinder worked marvelously.

A moon rose up, then broke into fragments.

The pleasure was augmented by fruity refreshments.

After they finished the rituals of welcome,

The Sials led the Kheras into their home.

---

to the court of Muslim Spain, from where they
were sent to the courts many European kings.
They evolved into gypsies.

In order to complete the tying of the knot,

Young girls were ready to do their part.

Mascara gave them an impish look.

The job of mocking the groom they undertook.

First girl   Your mother is an accursed piggy.

Second girl Your sister is going to dance for money.[1]

Third girl To hell with your best man.

Let him come and face us if he can.

Fourth girl Come, pay for the milk you drank,

  and be quick.

Your dilly dallying we won't let stick.

Fifth girl   You want our girl? The deal is uneven

Let your mother marry one of our servants.

To make the exchange equal.

That arrangement should do very well.

Narrator Young girls giggled, and pushed each other—

Twisted the groom's arm with all their power.

Indirectly they asked to be pampered

By their newly arrived family member.

They brought him a sugar pop as a treat,

---

[1]   Dancing to entertain professionally was
    considered a very low profession, because it
    was often associated with prostitution.

Declaring that's all he would get to eat.

The groom's sister and brother-in-law,

 as was the custom,

Lugged buckets of water for them.

Soon the lady-mullah arrived.

It was her job to ensure that the bride

Agreed to marriage willingly,

Was not coerced even slightly.

She did her job exceedingly poorly.

Narrator Each young girl wanted a ring for her pinkie.

They also demanded *the virgin bird's milky*,

And a packet of the blessed *marital sugar*

That ensures marital happiness forever.

They extracted the promise that in the wedding bed

He'd be gentle with the ring of the she-bird.

And find the paw of the golden hen.

Some wanted cash gifts there and then.

Groom O girl, doubtlessly you are an angel.

It doesn't suit you to begin with a quarrel.

King Solomon gave out three hundred rings,

Yet Balkis, his queen, held his heart's strings.[1]

---

[1] According to the legend popular among Punjabi Muslims, King Solomon had three hundred and sixty wives and concubines, but Queen Balkis was his true love. The identity of Balkis is not

As Solomon gave one to Balkis, I give you a
ring.
Monsoon is here, fair weather is in full swing.
Rain waters the soil, grass sprouts, the earth is green.
You too will make my arid life green.
With legs crossed I milked the cows, and filled
    up the milk vessel.
This should the milk of the virgin bird equal.
Red and green dress augments your beauty.
A fragrant essence exudes from your body.
I'm afraid my luck is not so good
To lie next to you in the glorious wedding bed.
The packet of *marital sugar* I'll certainly get you.
To begin, wear the jewelry I've brought you.
You walk so smoothly, as a duck gliding on the water.
When you speak, words come out like flowers.
Who among your girls seeks a consort?
I have brought men of an admirable sort.
In particular a few worthless men
Who would be happy to wed any woman.
All over the country is recognized our protector Saint;
Come, live among us, this is no time for restraint.
A fair is going on in our city—I have put up a tent.

---

established, but probably she is the queen of
Sheba.

Come, join us, enjoy the merriment.

You are wearing dark mascara,

Have reddened you lips with *dandasa*.[1]

Look in the mirror; don't doubt your beauty.

The fragrance of your body is spreading already.

You have asked for the impossible—they don't manufacture

The paw of the golden hen anywhere.

I searched all over and have brought you

Love that would never hurt you.

Bring a servant, and come with me.[2]

We would get along fabulously.

Narrator   Heer was drugged by her parents.

She talked to herself in half-awake moments.

Heer *(talking to herself)*   Why are they so intent
 on marrying me to Saida?

When God has already given me to Ranjha?

Why do they insist that I should sin—

When I'm already married, marry again?

It's like the Satanic trick, to give him water

And gain the thirsty man's soul in barter.

---

[1]Dandasa is an herb used by women to redden their lips
2. It was customary to send a female servant along
with the bride to stay with her for a few days to
      ensure her comfort.

Narrator   The honorable Kadi comes to perform
the wedding.

17. Kadi Advises Heer

Kadi   As a canon expert, I speak officially:
Obey the Shariah if you wish to be happy.
The reward is the Paradise when life is finished
If you keep your faith untarnished,
Maintain your modesty, eschew what's not kosher.
The rent of a sin is not mended ever.
Heer   Life is worth living, if by true faith it's led;
This world is ephemeral, so the sages have said.
Everything must perish, says the Quran.
My loving is vouchsafed by the Bull's horn.[1]
Kadi   On youth and beauty you mustn't depend.
You are too proud; your ways you should mend.
The Messenger taught that a Muslim must marry.
Come, do it; there is no reason to tarry.

---

[1]   It is a Hindu, not Muslim, belief that the earth is
held up by a bull on its horn, but early Muslim converts
kept many of the Hindu beliefs, which they used for
poetic purpose, much as English poetry uses Greek
Mythology.

Heer   The heart of a lover is a flower

heavenly.

You are treading on it heartlessly.

Why should I lose my faith just to save my life

Which, in any case, is full of strife?

Kadi   Per Shariah you'd receive skin-renting lashes.

I'd revive Omar bin Khatab's[1] justice.

When they see your fate, your friends would be

distraught.

Save them the pain; give up Ranjha's thought.

Close your eyes and bide your time.

This world is half clouds and half sunshine.

Heer   In the name of Shariah you institute tyranny,

Yet claim to be a friend of the citizenry.

Poor citizens couldn't be in worse predicament.

Bribes you accept, evil you foment.

I guess nothing is totally useless—God needs

fuel for the fire of the Hell.

You'd serve His purpose very well.

Kadi   Sinners would be handed back all their deeds.

They'd be thrashed according to their misdeeds.

---

[1] Omar was the second successor after Muhammad,
renowned for his justice. When his son was found
guilty of drinking, Omar gave him the same number
of lashes as he gave other similar offenders.

Into the fire they would be pushed,

The plebe as well as the distinguished.

When death comes, everyone goes alone.

Every purse is empty, every pocket torn.

Heer God has joined us in holy matrimony.

The Prophet himself performed the wedding ceremony.

Carefully we performed every rite proper.

Saint Qutb acted as the God-appointed lawyer.

To break up a union, and start another,

Tell me when God said it was kosher?

Meaning *Heer was truthful, did not lie,*

For in spirit she was married already.

True marriage results if God approves it.

Not if the ritual without love performed.

Kadi In the Quran it is clearly written:

Obedience to parents is a sacred obligation.

He who disobeys his mother or father

Is happy at first, but repents later.

He cries like the peacock when it sees its feet.[1]

The good that your parents do, no one can beat.

Heer I would marry Ranjha, my parents so promised.

This promise they later brazenly reneged.

---

[1] One of the Punjabi myths concerns the peacock. It
holds that when the peacock sees how ugly its feet are,
it is sad and loses its pride.

I promised Ranjha no one else I would marry.

I would keep this promise 'till I die.

Kadi They are closer to God who marry,

Obey their parents and accept matrimony.

A crow, when it thinks it is smart,

Is vulnerable, is likely to be shot.

Don't think you know what you are doing.

Listen to what your parents are saying.

Meaning *The parents and the Kadi talk mindlessly,*

Quote the Hadith and Quran glibly.

Their adages are facile, trite their refrain.

They speak God's name deliberately in vain.

Kadi *(to Choochak)* This stone is too hard to grind;

A more effective way we need to find.

Words are useless; you need measures severer.

Drug her more and also gag her.

I'd perform the rites, soon it would be over.

Or else this scandal would only grow stronger.

Narrator Heer guessed what was happening.

Loud was her crying and doleful her wailing

When they forced her into her *doli*[1]

And sealed the door after her tightly.

Heer O dear Father, I know you love me.

---

[1]A doli is a palanquin that is used to carry the bride.

Why are you letting them do this to me?

Don't you see they are carrying me away?

Stop them please, in your home let me stay.

Too short was my stay with you,

As if I only passed through

Your house—never lived in it—

And have no right to inhabit it.

I stayed under your roof as a wayfarer

Rests in the shade of a tree a short hour.

You never used to say no to me.

I was your pet, you adored me.

What has gone wrong; why have you forsaken me?

I was your darling; your affection had no limit.

Where has it gone? What happened to it?

Meaning This is the soul's darkest hour.

She is separated from the body;

And feels abandoned by God-

Father.

She appeals to His love, and does not understand

How he could let her down.

With Him she was once one;

And seeks a reunion, but to do so

It first must complete her mission on the earth:

Must complete loving the body.

The soul laments its present state,

Can't understand how God
Could let her down in the manner He did.

Heer O Ranjhan, I leave you to God's care.

What happens to me I no longer care.

How we planned, how we dreamed,

How wonderful the future seemed!

The dream world of our love lies shattered.

We have lost everything that to us mattered.

My heart is empty like a deserted palace.

No more I seek any comfort or solace.

18. Heer's Wedding

Narrator The Kadi forced the wedding; they
                     put her in her *doli*.

The Kheras planned to whisk her away stealthily.

Choochak gave her a rich dowry:

Horses, cattle, and boxes of jewelry.

The dowry made a spectacular show.

Heer screamed she didn't want to go.

All the community was in an uproar.

Such an outrage had never been seen before.

The Kheras stopped their celebrations and left

Like a thief leaving the place of theft.

Meaning   *The Heaven is sad, but does not act*

In order to give Heer and Ranjha the freedom
To fight their battle by themselves.

Narrator Feeling Ranjha's pain, the cows were upset[1]
Ran through the village, gored whoever they met.
Knocked down houses, raised a great din.
Stirred up so much dust, people couldn't see anything.

Meaning *The Providence saves Ranjha again.*

Narrataor People conjectured as to the cause
    of the catastrophe.

People It is certain Ranjha has been wronged.
Saida took what to Ranjha belonged.
Ranjha cursed us in his moment of torment.
An injured person's curse is most potent.
For sure Ranjha is the injured one.
Right away we should beg his pardon.

Narrator They besought him as if he were a Saint.
Most obsequious indeed was their plaint.
They danced around him, offered him delicious food,
Hoping to assuage his angry mood.
They did considerable begging and pleading,
Which Ranjha for a while kept resisting,
But finally they got him to agree
To take care of the cows, and save their property.

---

[1]Here the cows symbolize the divine wrath.

The Kheras traveled as fast as they could.

In the morning in front of their village they stood.

To welcome the bride, the girls sang merrily.

Heer was fed fried rice and some *choori.*[1]

Next her youngest brother-in-law, a toddling chap,

Was made to sit in the bride's lap.[2]

In the meantime, Ranja made a transformation—

Tore up his clothes, became a ghostly emanation.

Narrator   Heer and Ranjha send messages to each other.

Heer   O Ranjan, God knows my best I fought.

Now I am discouraged and feel distraught.

My life is slipping away; I watch helplessly.

They tied me up and forcibly abducted me.

Cruel were my parents, heartless the Kadi.

I fought them alone, I had no ally.

Alas, dear Ranjhan, 'tis the end of our liaison.

Still, my fight with the Kheras goes on.

Perhaps I might see you, God willing,

For now it is the end of everything.

Ranjha   From one's destiny one should not run.

You kept me poor; you are the cruel one.

---

[1]   Mushed bread, butter and sugar

[2]   This ceremony means that the bride promises
     that she would treat her youngest brother-in-
     law as her son.

You found a husband, left me alone.

Alone in my agony I moan and groan.

If you meant love to be temporary fun

You should've said so before it had begun.

You should not have so much encouraged me

If you were not capable of loyalty.

Heer Dear Ranjhan, there is a course open still.

Seek a guru: become his disciple,

Get your ears pierced, rub ashes over your body,

Come to see me in the guise of a yogi.

Meaning *The soul urges the body to become*
more spiritual.

19. Ranjha Vents

Narrator Choochak hung his head lower

When the Council discussed the matter,

And Ranjha cursed him like a sailor.

Ranjha The caliber of the Sials has fallen low.

They sell their daughters, even though

Their forehead has the mark of prostration[1]

[1]Those Muslims who pray regularly develop a callus
on their forehead, because the prayer includes
prostration. This callus identifies them as devout.

And their beards have a noble distinction.

Their daughters wear tinkling anklets,

Just as their cows wear tinkling bells

When they are taken to the market to be sold.

Their daughters are also available to be sold.

Good people, don't trust the word of a Jut.

It is broken as soon as it is said.

It has a very short life span,

Like a camel's footprint in the sand.

Twenty times a Jut must be abased

Before his friends accept him as a comrade.

When he sits on a pile of dirt he feels wiser.

(When he has stupid ideas, he thinks he is wiser.)

Aimlessly he wanders, like the dog of a butcher.

To avoid getting dirty, he doesn't sit on dirt,

But puts his turban between his haunch and dirt.

He weds his daughter to whoever comes by,

And steals from his son-in-law low and high.

He promises his daughter to one person.

Greed makes him give her to another one.

If you speak truth, they exile you.

Thieves and robbers are their who-is-who.

They let ugly crows rejoice in the tree,

But feed peacocks garbage only.

Narrator The ritual waiting ended,

the celebrations began.

The word got around, happy was every man.

The Kheras all danced and sang happily;

To congratulate them, the Khan[2] stopped by.

In Hazara people talked of Ranjha's affair.

His sisters-in-law gossiped with much flair.

They wrote him a letter inquiring how he was.

A dead man was asked how his health was.

Narrator His sisters-in-law send Ranjha a letter.

Letter What God decreed, happened; we feel your pain.

The news has opened our wounds again.

The flower that you tended with such tenderness

The Kheras plucked with a clever finesse.

For her sake you lived in that accursed place

Where lions and tigers are a known menace.

You can't trust these wily Sial lasses.

They let you down with ready excuses.

You toiled hard; your chances did not change.

We hope you'd listen to our refrain:

If a place hurts you, don't go there again.

You're welcome—all is not lost.

Come, live with us; there is no cost.

---

[2] A local chief higher than the tribal chief.

We'd offer gold at the shrine of a saint
If you ever come back to us again.
Ranjha *(writes back)*   O sisters, the butterfly
  remains hopeful,
Even when the autumn is most powerful,
That the flowers would bloom again—
The spring would bring another generous rain.
The nightingale keeps faith in the tree,
That once again fruitful it would be.
I have no hope of *the* spring coming again.
Exhausted and paralyzed I remain.
I wish to go to a place where
I'd find a friend with whom my pain to share.
I know the price of love is pain.
The cross is a part of this bargain.
I don't know why God is indifferent to me,
And what the purpose of His attitude might be.
In the dark remains the Will of the Light.[1]
Why he remains indifferent to my plight,
Never returns the life that is past,
Nor the luck that has been lost,
Nor the word spoken, nor the soul lost,

---

[1] Play of words: *the light remains in the dark.* Light
is one of the names of God. *In dark remains the will
of Light* means that the will of God remains unknown.

Nor an arrow from the bow shot.

If I keep returning to the same spot

It's because by love I am caught.

I lost my lands, also my beloved.

I have no choice but to get my ears pierced.[1]

Meaning The body means the body to seek

Spirituality;

The body seed it only as a ploy.

Narrator Heer's in-laws limited her freedom.

In-laws It seems quite prudent

To not let Heer visit her parents,

Lest the accursed servant latches on to her

And produce again a sick atmosphere.

Womankind, after all, is essentially frail.

It's possible in her duty Heer might fail.

20. A Newlywed Appears

Narrator It so happened that a young newlywed

Came to visit Heer, and this she said:

Meaning The Providence again intervened.

Newlywed I plan to visit my parents soon.

---

[1] Seek yoga

I hear that you hail from my hometown.

Your parents I would be able to see;

A message I would gladly carry.

Apprise your parents of how you are faring.

Tell me how your marriage is going.

Do your in-laws, as they should, love you?

How well does your husband treat you?

Share with me—newlyweds share with each other,

For we are forced to live among strangers

And have no trustworthy messenger.

Heer Here is my story in a few words: My silk
has moth infestation.

Newlywed I'm sorry; it sounds as if you are in a
    bad situation.

Heer When you reach the land of my birth

Lovingly kiss my beloved earth.

Spread your shawl on the ground.

Convey to my land my love profound. [1]

Tell it the heart-wrenching tale of my sorrow,

---

[1]Some understanding of the culture is needed to
understand this part of the poem. Clasping one's
hands and touching a person's feet are gestures of
intense love and devotion. A messenger can perform
 these   gestures on behalf of the sender of message.
These gestures can also express love of land of one's
    had Mother Earth to share her pain with.

How my evil parents chose an inferno
of an illegitimate marriage to send me to.
I was helpless; nothing I could do.
Also, on my behalf, please
Clasp your hands, touch Ranjha's feet,
And give him this message brief.

Heer's Message   I have been through hell
    and fire,
Have seen harrowed my every desire.
Unremitting is the pain of separation from you;
I have no zest for living, if it's without you.
Others are robbed in the dark of the night.
I was robbed in broad daylight.
The truth is that I'd rather be dead
Than live with my heart so crushed.

Meaning *The soul complains of separation
from the land to which the body is attached
emotionally.*
That is, the soul feels the body's pain.

Narrator   The newlywed reached her destination.
Right away she started her investigation.
Seeking a clue to Dhidu Ranjha,
A group of young girls finally she saw.

Newlywed *(to girls)* Who is this well-known servant
Who to the Sials by the Ranjhas was sent?

He is famous among champion lovers.

The crown of love he proudly wears.

Day and night for someone he pines,

Lives in the wilderness, visits holy shrines.

Love makes a mess of name and reputation.

Which house has suffered such devastation?

Girls   He's as good looking as he was ever.

When he lost Heer, he became a beggar—

Threw away his flute, shed this world's tangles.

Mindless of the dangers, he roams in jungles.

How he manages we don't really know.

Newlywed Please bring him to see me somehow.

Narrator The girls found Ranjha crazed with sorrow.

Girls *(to Ranjha)*   We think you would like to know

We have a message from a person dear to you.

Heer's Message   I gave up my home on

  account of you.

My pain is unbearable; come back to me

Disguised as a yogi, secretly.

The land of the Sial is cruel and unfair.

Why have you staked your tent there?

Ranjha *(responds)* You are living a life comfortable,

While on treacherous thorns I roll.

The fire of my pain is so intense

Were I to show how my heart burns

The firmament with its heat would glow.

The severity of my agony you do not know.

First you made me work as a servant.

Now you want me to be a mendicant.

I see your game: you would resurrect me

So that once again you might kill me.

Narrator Ranjha's words are cruel. Heer bides gracefully

The weight of the body the soul must carry.

Ranjha's message You are a newlywed,

 bathed in wedding hues.

Appealing to you is of no use.

You look innocent, but the truth is

In essence you are Tricky Kaido's niece.

Heer's message Dear Ranjhan, I miss you terribly.

Worse than hell is the Kheras' tyranny.

The pain is unbearable as it is.

With accusation please don't make it worse.

I am discouraged. I believe, however,

Death cannot be put off, nor the union of lovers.

O dearest, come back in the guise of a yogi.

No one would know your identity.

Come, gather your courage; be a resolute Jut.

Your Heer hasn't lost her fighting spirit.

Find a Guru, an accomplished yogi,

Who can help change our destiny.

Heer*(to the messenger)* Please bring this letter
 to my Ranjhan dear.

Meet him some place hidden from others.

Tell him how pain is eating at me.

I am near death, am a mere skeleton.

Before I die, please let me see you once.

Heer's Letter You said you liked my bangs.

My hair has changed; now it freely hangs

As long tresses, a cascade of curls.

Come, you might like the curls equally well.

My eyes you praised; they have not changed any.

Fragrant soap and *dandasa*—come and tell me,

Do they still make my face look pretty?

Meaning *The soul entices the body.*

Narrator Ranjha welcomed the messenger.

The messenger addressed Ranjha, in this manner:

Messenger It's not my business, but it must be
 said

The young lady, dear sir, is on her deathbed.

What kind of deception did you employ?

You hurt her so much, she wants to die?

The fragile little ship of her hope is floundering.

Noah's ark in a tempest is reeling.

The result of an unrequited love it is;

Not for a moment she has any peace.

She lives in the hope of seeing you, even
'though
You must have given her quite a severe blow.
If your name she utters it causes a battle.
Such is her life in the Kheras' castle.
Not for a moment does she stay in Khera's bed.
Sits in the window, waits for you instead.
She has, dear sir, troubles plenty;
Do as she bids you: become a yogi.

Meaning *Through the messenger, the soul*
   indirectly chastises the body.

   Ranjha *(to the messenger)* My dear Heer's
   message makes me distraught;
Dark are my feelings, doleful my thought.

Ranjha's Letter The stream of my pain flows
 turbulently.
I became a fakir when you dazzled me.
I put on line everything I had.
With dark sorrow, now I am going mad.
Pain and suffering you've bequeathed me;
Yourself found comfort in marital safety.

Meaning *Ranjha still does not comprehend*
The spiritual nature of his pursuit.

Ranjha *(musing)* Within my reach is my dear Heer.
I need to overcome my baseless fear.

If I dare reach out, I can win her.

I would have to renounce my pride and honor.

Freely He dispenses it: love is God's gift.

It's good to be greedy, aggressively seek it.

The life of a fakir I am already living.

Everything I have I am already sacrificing.

Still, the game of love I am losing.

There must be something I'm forgetting.

Meaning   *Ranjha has some intimation of the*
   nature of his pursuit.

He needs to set his house on fire

 Burn each and every desire.

Lose himself, and find the object of his desire.[1]

Ranjha *(musing)* The embers of my love are still hot;

The fire of love I should restart.

Narrator   He chose as his teacher the Guru Balnath.

Eagerly he started on his path.

Ranjha *(musing)* My hair I should get shaved.

---

[1] This is a Sufi thought. To find God, one must
first lose one's own self (all desires other than
 love for Him), which, I believe, has much the
same meaning as the Christian concept of
emptying one's soul. The poet means that the
love between Heer and Ranjha is a secular
representation of the love between Man and
God, and makes similar demands.

Pierce my ears and thus be saved.

Put on copper rings, discard gold.

Devote myself to a goddess bold

Who'd teach me how to steal a woman.

No other way my job can be done.

21.Ranjha Seeks Yoga

Narrator Ranjha went around calling forth aloud.

Ranjha Come, good people, have no doubt.

Come, and you would find peace.

Come and live among holy yogis.

Your food you'd beg; no work you'd need to do.

Forget cultivating and herding too.

Get your ears pierced, rub ashes over your body

To advise people then you would be ready.

You'd worry about no birthday presents.

Free you would be of all worldly torments.

'Give nothing, receive nothing,

Own nothing and owe nothing,'

Would be your guiding principle.

You would never need to attend a funeral.

Meaning *Ranjha still has a very poor*
   understanding of the nature of his mission.

Narrator Ranjha reached Balnath in due time.

Humbly he pleaded:

Ranjha O Yogi Sublime!

Please accept me as your new pupil.

To you I surrender my free will.

Enlighten me with your wise instruction.

I've given up every worldly possession.

I sought Truth; it dawned on me

You are the proper teacher for me.

Remove my shackles; please make me free.

Show me the way to spiritual liberty.

Narrator The guru saw Ranjha, and
  immediately kenned

That he was rather a haughty person.

Good looking, a dandy, an epicure

Of pleasurable things, a good connoisseur,

A pet of his parents, spoiled to the marrow,

Is seeking to forget his pain and sorrow,

Has gotten entangled in an amorous mess.

Balnath Tell us the truth; what brings you to us?

Ranjha I've realized this world is ephemeral.

I see it crumble like a wall of sand.

All happiness is transient, short lasting,

Like a cloud in the sky passing.

---

[1] Muslim believe that the angel Izrael comes to
the dying person to fetch his soul.

In the end Izrael[1] scoops up us all.

We are the lords, but soon we shall fall.

When all is done and over, in dust we sink,

Even if the Elixir of Life we drink.

Balnath Bracelets around your wrists, rings
   in your ears tinkling,

A *lungi*[2] round your legs loosely hanging:

They suit you very handsomely.

Shoulders covered by a shawl—you're quite a dandy.

Scented hair, mascara in your eyes—you
   must have some money.

You are likable, but the truth is

The likes of you don't make yogis.

It is difficult to deny life's pleasures.

The Guru gets blamed for the disciple's failures.

The path of the yogi is not for everyone.

Why enter the battle that's not likely to be won?

Your course in life is very different.

Play your flute, sing, enjoy women,

Eat what you like, keep your body clean,

Keep to herding and cow-milkin'.

A mundane life you should be living.

Tell me the truth, what are you really seeking?

---

[2]A kilt-like wrap garment worn by men around their legs.

Ranjha   I said goodbye to this world, the
 home of travail,

Where corrupt dealings and treachery prevail.

You gain nothing but constant frustration,

Win nothing but perpetual degradation.

The entry to the Land of Bliss he only wins

Who curbs the urges of the Five Sins.

Please help me gain salvation.

I come seeking your benediction.

Balnath   With the Ultimate Source, yoga began.

The tradition of yoga is not easy to maintain.

You begin with eating tasteless food.

Next you taste the bitterest gourd.

The world of a novice is a funeral pyre

Ready to burn his every desire.

The ashes that he rubs over his body

Are the ashes of his instincts rowdy.

There is no place for any resistance—

No room for the slightest hubris.

Ranjha You teach me the Way; I'm ready to learn.

Lust and greed are the fires that burn.

I need *fukr*[1] to put the fires out.

---

[1] *Fukr i*s the state or practice of being a fakir. The
reader should note that the poet uses the words
Yoga (a Hindu concept) and *fukr,* a Muslim

I need the faith that kills every doubt.

Nothing has permanence; all riches are ephemeral.

A servant without pay, I am your disciple.

Balnath Difficult is the yogi's way of living.

You start the day with conch-sounding.

Conscientiously you must concentrate on breathing,

Raise it to the highest level of being.

Master your emotions—no happiness over a birth

Nor sadness over a dear friend's death.

Wash your hair, dry it in the sun,

Only to strew in ashes again.

Keep your distance from all men.

Although they are pretty, never look at women.

Opium and marijuana keep you in bliss.

They make up the loss; no happiness you miss.

All existence is a dream, all thinking foolishness.

Have no illusions; renounce cleverness,

Live in wilderness, don't forget pilgrimages.

Regularly perform ablution in the Ganges.

Pay homage to the yogis holier than you.

O Jut, Yoga would be too hard for you.

You ogle women, live a life of reveling,

But yoga is for those who've given up everything.

---

concept, interchangeably, implying that essentially
they are the same.

Ranjha Be kind enough to give me the boon;

I earnestly hope that you do it soon.

A good deed should not come belated.

Accept me; I would be forever indebted.

Balnath You have to learn to ride the Steed of
 Patience,

And be guided by God's remembrance,

And curb the lower, rebellious desire,

Which you must burn with devotion's fire.

You risk your life if you seek *Fukr*.

The faint of heart can't scale this tower.

Meaning *Ranjha uses the words that sound just right*
The yogi knows the Jut's speech is trite.

Balnath Have you learned what you first have to learn?

The lamp of devotion in your heart must burn.

Of death you must not be afraid.

Always remember the adage

The body that is pure can host the Divine Being.

He is All; He is in everything. [1]

Through the beads of the rosary runs one string.

So the Invisible weaves through everything.

Everything under the sun has an essence:

Living beings have life; opium has its illusory

---

[1]   "He is everything," is a Muslim axiom. "He is in everything" is a Hindu one.

experience;

Bright red color is green henna's essence;

The essence of human life is holy experience,

Which engenders spirituality

As the blood engenders physical vitality.

Narrator Ranjha was intent on becoming a yogi.

To dissuade him, the Guru did everything.

Unable to change the petitioner's mind,

The Guru felt sad, decided to be kind.

Accepted Ranjha as a disciple.

Other disciples didn't take this very well.

It created an uproar among his followers.

They sharpened their tongues—attacked

 him with oral daggers.

Disciples His fair skin makes you accept the newcomer.

Long have we worshiped; to us you are unfair.

Alas! Even yogis fall for fair boys.

Even the holy have lost their poise.

Meaning *The trainee yogis renounce their faith readily,*

Faith losing its hold on humanity.[1]

Balnath *(to his disciples)* Malicious backbiting

 and spiteful lies,

---

[1] Here Waris Shah bemoans the loss of religiosity
among yogis, therefore Hindus, but he obviously
means that all religions are losing their potency.

I have warned you, are common frailties.

You have to be careful; you must make sure

You are not guided by reason immature.

I don't have yoga tied to my neck.

(I do not monopolize it.)

You are free to find it yet.

In the end I'd leave it behind me.

Why are you acting so impatiently?

Narrator The disciples got excited, became riotous—

Knocked the Guru down, left him helpless.

Took off their hoods, threw away their rings;

Gave back the guru every sacred thing.

In one body they deserted the precincts—

Decided to quit, led by low instincts.

Narrator   Ranjha rose and came to Guru's aid.

Quite a convincing speech he made.

Ranjha Desolate would be the lives of those

   who are mean to me.

I have no worry, for God is good to me.

If you think calmly, you would not oppose me.

I bring you friendship; what have you against me?

Let's settle this matter peacefully,

For using force is an act dastardly.

If someone spoils a poor man's affair,

Gently we should remind him to be fair.

If a boat is sinking, bring it ashore.

Don't let it sink because you dislike its oars.

If you want a good deed done,

Do it now; don't let it drag on.

Balnath Humans tend to foster enmities,

Try to pull wool over each other's eyes.

The Jut's speech is candid, though not witty.

His guilelessness has earned my sympathy.

Put on your rings; stop this foolishness.

Truth lovers are not afraid of the cross.

Narrator The disciples obeyed; their salvation
 was rescued.

Every mantra in their repertoire they used.

Many atoning rituals they eagerly completed.

Three hundred sacred shrines they visited.

With many super-Gurus they humbly pleaded.

In obtaining forgiveness they finally succeeded.

Within four days they fixed up their rings,

Also took back their discarded things.

Next they destroyed Ranjha's silken clothing

To prepare him for the rite of anointing.

For the occasion they showed great fervor:

To re-shave Ranjha they obtained a new razor.

Narrator The Guru told his disciples he would ordain

Ranjha a yogi—their opposition would be in vain.

Balnath had Ranjha sit by his side

And swear that he had renounced his pride.

And lust and greed he had mastered,

Which was evidenced by his ears pierced.

The news spread over the land rapidly

That Ranjha had become an ordained yogi.

Balnath Be mindful of God every moment.

You'd then understand what the training rituals meant.

Exchange your clothes for tattered raiment.

Do not seek any other adornment.

Carry nothing but a bowl and a conch.

All precious possessions you must scorn.

Find a village where you sing your hymns.

Hymns, remember, drive away sins.

Prayers cleanse human abodes.

For a yogi they are spiritual roads.

By begging you must gain all your bread.

The older woman you should treat like your mother,

The younger one as your sister.

Narrator For the guru Ranjha had something
in store.

To the Guru, thus he spoke:

Ranjha Come, Yogi, don't push me around.

Your advice does not seem very sound.

You yourself should swallow it.

If I take it, I would vomit.

First you castrate your disciples,

Then teach them yoga principles.

Come, tell me briefly what you have to say.

I don't have time to listen to you all day.

Balnath   Brother, it is now understood,

You have accepted a load on your head.

The thought of unloading you must dread.

From now on, this is how you must earn your bread:

To eat you must beg your food

One piece at a time, or it is no good.

A whole meal you must never gather.

Never eat the food that's not kosher.

Be content even if you only eat a little.

In every way possible, make yourself humble.

Never enjoy a woman's sight.

Always wear your underwear tight.

Ranjha   If I could have kept my underwear tight

Why would I have my present plight?

To curb my desires if I was able,

Why would I cause myself so much trouble?

If I could control my wild passion

Why would I fight battles that have no termination?

A beauty drove me—she was inexorable,

Or I would've never given you this trouble.

If I had thought it would injure my pride
I wouldn't have shaved, nor exposed my hide.
If I had known the nature of your dealings
I would've never worn your earrings.
If I had known you ban all laughter
I would've never come near your quarter.
I joined you to gain a certain end
Which does not cause in my pride a dent.
I might even demand you fix my ears,
And take you to court—this you should fear.
Meaning   *Ranjha is no fakir,*
He is loyal to no one except his Heer.
Balnath   Only eat what's kosher.
The word that's not true, never utter.
Renounce your affair clandestine.
Repent while still there is time.
If you repent, your sins would be forgiven.
Give up your habits of pagan origin.
Plug up moral loopholes; leave none open.
Likely, her fling the Jutti has forgotten.
She is happily taking care of her husband.
Others tend the cows that only you could tend.
You wanted to reach your goal stealthily:
Give up your tricks, seek humility.
You invested nothing, but want dividends.

In a disaster your business would end.

I thought I saw your humility.

I granted you the earrings trustingly.

Ranjha O 'Natha,[1] I am alive and you want
   me to die!

It's too much, for a passionate man am I.

I am a Jut; I lasso cattle.

I do not handle delicate crystal.

You pierced my ears; that's enough insult.

Don't you understand I belong to a different cult?

I don't waste time on caring for a bowl.

To me it's only a receptacle for dole.

In the end, one and the only hassle

I accept is taking care of the cattle.

The teacher who teaches that I give up women,

In my estimation is a simpleton.

If someone insults me I should do nothing?

Such saintliness, dear sir, is not my thing.

Balnath *(to himself)* An ass does not pray
very well

Even if it puts on a saint's apparel.

---

[1]In a familiar address, Balanath changes to Natha. It
shows that Ranjha no longer accepts their
relationship to be that of a guru and a disciple, but
considers himself Balnath's peer.

I should not expect much from a Jut.

I can't make him what he is not.

Meaning   *Ranjha has his eyes on what's visible.*

In Heer he seeks something invisible.

Ranjha wears no saintly apparel,

But prays well, because he loves well.

Ranjha The thought of yoga came to me

When I fell in love with a young lady.

I found pleasure, as a child finds a toy.

We were young, got drunk with joy.

Her parents promised her hand to me.

I was as happy as I could be.

When it came to money, things got harried.

Her parents decided to another she should be married.

They reneged their promise; to a Khera

 she was betrothed.

When trouble mounted, you I approached.

You must know love is a ruthless power.

Even the prophets it does not spare.

Ayub's[1] bones rotted forsaken, and Yacub[2] cried

in despair.

In love's path, no better you fare.

---

[1]Muslim's hold Ayyub to be an old
Testament prophet. He is probably Jonah.
[2]Prophet Jacob, father of Joseph.

Love drove me to hypocrisy—

I didn't do it deliberately.

That is why I do not feel guilty.

Narrator His eyes closed, Balnath invoked

  God's presence,

And started to pray for Ranjha's deliverance.

Balnath You do as You would; we mortals have no say.

 You created everything, you do as you may.

A simple minded Jut has a high aspiration—

He seeks Love's true benediction.

Deep and sincere is his devotion to his Heer.

Which has led him to adopt the guise

   of a holy fakir.

He means to deception.

He did what he did, because of his devotion.

He has given up his name and clan.

He aspires to be good—he does what he can.

You are the last hope of the crestfallen.

If anyone can help him, only You can.

Please heed the request of this meek yogi.

Let it be known what Your will might be.

Narrator   Balnath received a divine intimation

That Ranjha would reach his destination.

Meaning *Banath means that Ranjha would*

   reach his spiritual goal.

But the body thinks only of his carnal goal.

Balnath Dear child, I bring you good news.

The battle of love you will not lose.

The object of your desire is now yours.

The sapling that you planted now bears flowers.[1]

Ranjha braced up; to leave he got ready.

Gladly to everyone he said goodbye.

22. Ranjha Leaves Balnath

Narrator   So eager was he to say goodbye

He flew like a falcon in his mind's eye.

Seeing Ranjha so readily fulfilled,

Balnath's disciples were chagrined.

Ranjha *(to the disciples)* You find yoga if it is
 so destined.

You do not get it if you are out of luck.

I am a Jut; my asset is my pluck.

I have no understanding or sophistication.

God took pity on my situation.

Do not lose hope so readily.

----

[1]   Balnath does not provide false hope. He means
that Ranjha would obtain his spiritual goal.

You too would be fulfilled by and by
When God looks at you graciously.
You would get your share fortuitously.
Man has no claim, for God owes him nothing.
No right has man to ask for His blessing.
Except that His very nature is loving,
It's no imposition if we ask for His blessing.
Remember fate is a two faced doctor:
With one hand he kills, with the other cures.
Narrator Down the hill he ran;
 nothing barred his way.
As Monsoon washes clean the hillside, so he washed
 his worries away.
Calling upon God, he challenged his foe,
'Though the art of fighting he did not know.
Bravely he advanced, buoyed by soldierly spirit,
Ready for a fight, his hand on the hilt.
His imaginary sword was better than the real;
The coming victory he already could feel.
He moved speedily toward Kheras' land
Like a brave general in full command—
Or a hungry lion chasing its prey,
Or a thief from the site of theft running away.
With roused desire he moved on,
A raindrop at the head of a windstorm.

Wherever he went people wondered:

People This yogi is too young; why has he entered

The sect of yogis, when he could do better?

His earrings are too big, his dress out of kilter.

We do not think he would last much longer.

Ranjha For seven generations, our ancestors

  have been fakirs.

Of our capabilities you should have no fears.

Never were we a farmer; our name is

 Sorrow Expunger.

We are the grandson of the Great Doctor.

He who foolishly distrusts us

For the rest of his life would be childless.

23. Sheep Herder

Narrator Ranjha entered a town, where he saw

 a sheep-herder

Who stared at him and came over closer.

Trying to identify him, he said in a whisper,

Sheep Herder You can't hide a thief or a gossiper,

Or the identity of a lover.

What's going on? Are you really a fakir?

Ranjha We are the citizens of Lanka, dear sir.

On our way we are to the festival of Hardwar.

It has been a very difficult journey
Because we had to cross a vast sea.
Twelve years we spent meditating,
Another twelve years peregrinating,
Observing the wonders of the nature.
Herder   You are a servant of a Jut for sure.
For years you herded Choochak Sial's cows.
Come, this story everyone knows.
With a pretty Jutti you had an affair,
Although for her you did not care.
Poor Heer earned the community's scorn.
You'd better disappear as soon as you can.
The Sials are going crazy with anger.
To bring you to your demise they are eager.
Ranjha   Herding is no doubt a noble profession
But you, dear friend, are following the Satan.
While herding sheep you also besmear
The name of this poor meek fakir.
Fakirs are like snakes black.
It won't do if you paint them black.
Herder   For Sials you did herding and milking.
When in trouble, you went yoga seeking.
Heed my advice; go back, you Jut.
Stop this tactless conniving act.
You've smeared ashes all over your face.

You claim to be a yogi, but don't look me in the
face.
You are the well-known Ranjha the Lover.
Your pierced ears you use as a cover.
A Khera wedded Heer; you lost your honor.
Shamelessly you went on living, however.
You watched while they carried her away.
Your beard they shaved;[2] not a word did you say.
One should not bow to one's enemy.
Everyone agrees you acted cowardly.
When you had no trick left any more
You decided to knock at Balnath's door.
If you think your honor you can retrieve
By using a new trick, you are naïve.
When called, you didn't rise to the occasion.
You went into hiding, took no action.
You are ignorant if you do not comprehend
Your life has already come to an end.
The Sials would certainly lop off your head
If they see you anywhere near their stead.
Ranjha For seven generations, we have been yogis,
We own nothing but a bowl and a rosary.
This world for us has no meaning,

---

[2]To shave someone's beard means to insult him/her
publicly.

Our only livelihood is begging.

Do or don't we look like a fakir?

Who is this Ranjha and who is Heer?

The names mean nothing to us, dear sir.

Don't you see the signs of a deliverer?

Yoga perfection we've attained, dear sir.

A Jut and a servant you say we are.

I could tear you to pieces, my dear sir.

Narrator   With anger Ranjha was furiously seething.

His eyes in his head were violently rolling.

Herder   O Reverend Yogi, forgive me my sin.

You've come from across a great ocean.

Excuse me. I didn't see your exalted station.

Narrator   The herder spoke sarcastically—

Enjoyed his own words enormously.

Herder   Bringing his food was just an excuse.

To see her Ranjhan, she used that clever ruse.

Happily together they enjoyed frolicking,

Fostered a love madly intoxicating.

He played his flute; she came following.

Their passions were inflamed; their

 world was enchanting.

As milk fresh from the cow's udder

Has its unique and pleasing flavor,

So was uniquely intoxicating

The young lovers sensuous frolicking.

It was a life worth a life sacrificing.

By and by came the time of her wedding.

She would not wed voluntarily,

In a *doli* they put her forcibly.

She got married, he remained single.

His days and nights turned doleful.

With her husband went the husband's darling.

The herder's gear he was left holding.

Come, dear friend, get going, or else

The Sials would descend on you like a curse.

I tell you the truth, you cannot win

This business, my friend, cannot be kept hidden.

Narrator Ranjha finally admitted his disguise.

Ranjha   A wise bunch are you sheep-herders.

Plato is among your wise ancestors.

Deep like a sage is your vision,

Sharp like the talon of a falcon.

Dear friend, I commend you on your observation.

I beg you treat it with circumspection.

It is not manly to betray a secret.

A real man's mouth remains ever shut.

He keeps secrets in confidence,

Unlike a crow with no continence

That lets out its turd anywhere.

Tattling diminishes your own honor.

Herder You started the affair; you should have
 eloped with her.

You have besmeared lovers' honor.

If another was going to wed her

Why did you undertake this adventure?

What has it done to your honor?

Heer is with a Khera; you hang on to life.

What a shame! You should have ended your life.

O you naive, poor, innocent sinner.

Why so much ado—you've already lost honor?

Ranjha   If they espy someone's infraction,

Good men like to use circumspection,

Do not shame the perpetrator.

They know infamy is an unbearable horror.

Even if a thief cleans them out

They give him the benefit of the doubt.

On a perilous journey I embark.

I fear my arrow might miss its mark.

A thief or robber might give up his vocation.

No true lover ever gives up his devotion.

Herder Come, I was only joking; don't mind
my kidding.

Play your tricks,.go all out avenging.

Love is a fire irrepressible.

No one can extinguish it very well.
People are engaged in malicious gossip.
It is time for yourself you stood up.
Everything has its time proper:
The swoop of a hawk, the trick of a swindler.
So the union of lovers has its rhyme.
You cannot gain it before its time.
Go pick up your girl; take her to your town.
It won't bother me. I mind business my own.
The Kheras are no kin or kith of mine.
Whatever you do is with me just fine.

24. Khera Country

Narrator The sheep-herder swore secrecy.
Reassured, Ranjha proceeded directly
To the Khera town, traveling impatiently.
Soon he found himself in the Khera country.
Ranjha (in a marketplace) O good people,
 what is this country?
Who is its chief? What town is it?
Who are the people who've settled it?
How long has this land been habited?

Excuse me, I come here uninvited.

Narrator A few young girls were standing nearby.

When they heard him, loudly they cried:

Girls We think Heer's friend we see.

Narrator But no one could tell his identity.

He drank from a well, sat down under a tree

As if from all cares he was free.

Girls   This place is called Color Town.

Meaning *The town is all show, no substance.*

Narrator He laughed at the name, as if he saw a clown.

Gently he approached the girls, and asked politely,

Ranjha   Who is your chief? Is he generous or miserly?

Girls The chief is Ajju Khera. Saida is his son;

Ranjha's property he sits on.

Narrator   Ranjha picked up his conch and bowl,

Said he was going to take a stroll.

Sideways he reeled; back and forth he swayed.

Sometime he sighed; other times he prayed.

The girls followed him, talking genially,

Asked him the name of his country.

The yogi went into a spiritual trance,

Engaged in a clumsy and awkward dance.

Ranjha The Kheras are a tribe most wonderful.

The young girls here are most beautiful.

Men who love them in the end repent.

They are disloyal, 'though they look innocent.

Girls   O holy seer,

You are unfair.

Narrator The girls returned home quite excited.

Girls   O mother, a new yogi we have sighted.

Often he is in a trance, lost in prayer.

Many colorful rings in his ears he wears.

His beard and head he has shaved.

Whoever follows him is saved.

Sometimes wild flowers grow in the city.

He happens to be in our vicinity.

Sweet as honey is his nature.

If you deny him food, he smiles the more.

His necklace and earrings are quite colorful.

Certainly they suit him exceedingly well.

With love his eyes seem intoxicated.

To his vocation he appears devoted.

Of divining the future he has many ways;

Many chants and different mantras he says.

Sometimes iron chains he scatters.

In the dust sometimes he draws odd figures.

Sometimes he laughs, sometimes weeps.

God's name is always on his lips.

High must he his teacher's station.

We do not doubt true is his devotion.

Narrator Sehti came home and spoke so:

Sehti O Sister, a new yogi has come to our place.

Handsomely he wears his rings and necklace.

Ashes he has smeared all over his body;

Perhaps he is not a genuine yogi.

I suspect he is looking for a gem that he has lost.

One moment he sings, next he is distraught.

In his bearing he is a rajah's son.

He is handsomer than any of our men.

He wanders singing, lost in his thought.

You can't tell if he is a real yogi or not.

He examines closely the face of every person,

The married as well as the unmarried one.

He hasn't yet found whoever he's looking for,

But remains persistent in his endeavor.

Perhaps he is the victim of love unrequited.

Why else has he himself so outfitted?

Meaning *Whether fate brought him,*

or of his own he came,

There is no doubt the yogi has an aim.

Which is a part of the Divine aim,

The knowledge of which no mortal can claim.

Heer   O sister, that's a sad subject.

Completely it fuddles my intellect.

When I heard you mention a yogi,

The ground slipped from under me.

With sympathy for him my heart is aching.

I wonder how he manages to goes on living

After he had his ears pierced.

In painful thoughts I am immersed.

My sorrow is deep, raven black

Many painful memories come rushing back.

You just mentioned a young man.

Where is from? Tell me if you can.

Who was she who forsook him?

Took away his smile and his eyes' gleam?

He has no friends to give him solace

When life is hard, and the world is callous.

Meaning *The soul worries about the body*
What trials and tribulations did it go through?

Heer *(to herself)*   I hope this yogi is my Ranjhan.

I cannot see him; I am heartbroken.

Painful enough was our separation.

Now that he is near, it's beyond toleration.

Meaning *God made the soul such,*
Ever so near the body, yet inaccessible.

Narrator   Heer cried alone, hid herself from others.

Her eyes shed copious torrents of tears.

Meaning *The burden of true love, the lover*
      carries alone.

Heer *(to girls)* Make an excuse; get the yogi in here.

Together we can ask him he comes from where

And why; wearing ashes, he roams all over.

Is there a secret under his cover?

Why does he trudge places so doggedly?

What is it that he really wants to see?

Why has he come to the Khera estate?

Is it fate or an act deliberate?

Narrator The girls came back to see the yogi.

They paid their respects, and said respectfully,

Girls   We come to you to do what's right.

To us you have brought your sacred light.

With your presence our town is blessed,

Which means you are our holy guest.

Per our custom we owe you hospitality.

It'd be a shame if we forgot our duty.

Please be our guest, do us a favor:

Come to Heer's home and kindly bless her.

Ranjha   We eat little, need no food.

At social conversation we are no good.

To the Festival of Khomb we are going.

We live on the food that we gain by begging.

Girls Don't flout the custom; accept the invitation.

Please pay attention to our situation.

It would be for us quite embarrassing
If in vain is our inviting.
A brief tour of Ajju Khera's yard,
And a few words with Heer—that should not
 be very hard.
The home of the Chief you'd get to see.
Also his daughter, pretty Sehti.
Come, don't be too proud, though you're a holy man;
The Kheras, after all, are not a lowly clan.
Ranjha   In the realm of *fakiri* we are veterans.
We've practiced it for seven generations.
No regard we have for the customs of this world.
In the wild we live like a bird.
In the wild we must make our abode.
No need we have for a street or a road.
It doesn't matter if you are beautiful,
For we think only they are beautiful
Who find yoga through Divine Grace.
The soul is too restless to live in one place.
Never would we be a city inhabitant.
Always in the forest we stake our tent.
Girls *(to each other)* This yogi is
   unique, rather squeamish;
His gaze is charming, gestures stylish.
Pretty earrings he wears, and a befitting necklace.

A bowl and a conch he carries every place.

His darting eyes and his lips that quiver

Betray him, 'though his mien is quite sober.

He makes excuses to keep his eyes closed.

There is something he doesn't want disclosed.

Girls *(to Ranjha)* Who charmed you?

   Where is your country?

Why have you chosen the life of a yogi?

You've got to tell us what the truth is.

At this young age, you made promises

That forced you to accept ascetic yoga.

Are you a victim of the hate of a sister-in-law?

You are very much the talk of this town.

All of your story is already known.

When young girls in a group gather

They talk of you in a hushed whisper.

Come, sweetheart, let's do it.

Let's not make a hassle of it.

You are wise, don't you see.

We won't leave until you agree?

Ranjha   A lion, a black snake, and a yogi

Belong never to any country.

Like birds we travel from one land to another

We are not tied to one place forever.

Wherever we are, that's our country,

And Yoga is our caste practically.

No relations or tribesmen we have anymore,

Nor any friend, nor a paramour.

What good is holding up boulders with glue?[1]

Your efforts to detain me will not do.

Narrator The girls persisted, refused to leave his side.

The yogi acted as if he were peeved.

Ranjha   Please, dear girls, don't annoy the yogi.

With you we do not wish to be angry.

We are afraid of our own power.

If angry, we'd be a ghost with evil power.

Why should we visit any chief or leader?

The truth is we do not even care

To pee on this wonderful land of theirs.

Their worldly power we do not fear.

Girls We approached you earnestly, for

A representative of holy Balnath you are.

We invited you most sincerely.

But you're not pleased; rather, are angry.

We offered that our chief you might see.

---

[1]   This line has four meanings. 1. The girls are too weak to change the yogi's mind. 2. The worldly customs and traditions cannot prevent the Yogi's pursuit of Truth. 3. Everyone must die; it is futile to fight death. 4. Materialistic customs and traditions cannot suppress spiritual life for very long.

You have chosen to not agree.

(You have treated us rudely.)

Ranjha   There is no doubt you are beautiful.

In my heart I also know full well

The beautiful ones are also critical.

You would find fault with an angel.

To different realms belong you and we:

You are pinioned to the world earthly;

We reside in that unknown place

Which lies beyond the world sensate.

For the sake of God, now be silent.

You'd never understand our predicament.

You girls are naive if you believe

We are free to stay or leave.

We are not free to accept your invitation.

Our vows put us in this situation.

To go begging we were ready.

You have detained us mischievously.

We've killed our attachments worldly.

You try to resurrect them, though innocently.

We have thrown off the yoke eternal.

You direct us back to the well.[1]

---

[1] A yoked ox is a slave to the well—is bound to hauling its water. A lusty person is a slave to lust. The well, here, has the same meaning as

The tangle of desire we've shed, but

You lead us to the same entrapping net.

We are ready to go begging.

Why do you object to our leaving?

Narrator He picked up his bowl, started on his way

Different people received him in different ways.

First Woman Here is little something for you to eat:

Bread and butter, and a piece of meat.

Ranjha We cannot accept it; it is a plateful

Please give us just a morsel.

Second Woman A yogi! How propitious!

Please, revered Yogi, pray for us.

Third Woman You fake! You have been

drinking heavily.

You look at young women brazenly.

Fourth Woman You are casing our house, you robber.

It is our money that you are after.

Ranjha Here we are in this town; per chance

Young girls here don't sing, nor do they dance.

No games any children are playing,

---

siren in Greek mythology. I might also point out
the meaning of Ranjha's refusal to see Heer. Since
he is seeking Heer, it does not make sense that he
should let go of an opportunity to see her. The
refusal means that Ranjha does not want a social
visit.

Nor is there any dust flying.

(Your town is vapid and mirthless.

We could not care for it any less.

It is spiritually exiguous.)

Girls   Come, we will show you, dear yogi,

The places where young girls sing happily.

They dance entranced, sing rapturously

While they also weave diligently.

Narrator   The women of the area a meeting arranged,

All and every caste the guests ranged.

Some were pretty, dressed very well;

Others were not so very beautiful.

Some were perfumed heavily.

Others wore scent more naturally.

Some were laden with ornate jewelry.

They all surrounded Ranjha cleverly,

Engaged him in a pleasant conversation

And steered him to their location.

First woman How handsome he is!

Second woman How beautiful are his eyes!

Third woman You cannot trust these handsome men.

Readily they love, readily they run.

Narrator One of them wiped his ash-soiled face

Put her face close to his face.

Fourth woman   O dear yogi, name your wish.

Would you like a delicious dish?

Narrator   Sehti too acted coquettishly—

Removed his necklace seductively.

Ranjha   You naughty girl, who are you?

Women   She is the daughter of the Chief Ajju.

Ranjha   Ajju, Bhajju, Pajju, Fujju,[1]

They are all one and the same.

I don't care what's the Chief's name.

Ajju has raised a daughter rebellious.

The result of it might be disastrous.

A gentle yogi she greeted with sass.

Rudely she took off his holy necklace,

Did not abstain from hitting him.

Freely she indulges her every whim,

Prances around like a young, wild mare.

The weaving room she won't come near.

So far it's neither here nor there.

What she'd next do Ajju should fear.

Sehti   Watch out, if I ever catch you

 I would make a lathering mush of you.

You would then learn a lesson new,

How I handle the likes of you.

Your limbs I would break into pieces.

---

[1] Ranjha makes fun of the name Ajju.

You would then know what justice is.

If you come my way, I'd skin you alive.

You'd be glad if I leave you alive.

I'd thrash you as they thrash donkeys.

You would forget all your trickeries.

If you come begging at my door

I would have something special in store.

Ranjha You are as dangerous as a snake and a lion;

You eat flesh,[1] suck blood human.[2]

No reason you have for quarreling with us.

What is the use of carrying on thus?

Forbear and forgive; may God bless you.

Grant your parents a long life too.

Don't give my heart any more pain.

A sin you'd earn, nothing good you'd gain.

O daughter luck-ful,[2] precious golden goose,

I hope you do not your good luck lose.

You vanquisher of men, perhaps you would find

---

[1] Meaning, you eat un-kosher meat.

[2] To suck human blood means to exploit others to
the point of killing them.

[1] In Punjabi, the word hungry also means low class and mean
person. To call someone hungry is an insult.

[2] When a young girl is addressed as luck-ful, it means: 1) The speaker hopes and
wishes that she has a good fortune; 2) The speaker has innocent intentions in
approaching the girl.

A lover who matches your own tough mind.

Narrator Ranjha started his begging round.

The open door of a house he found.

A Jut was milking a cow happily.

Ranjha tooted his conch forcefully

And entered the house like a charging bull.

"God is!" He shouted in a voice forceful.

The cow got spooked; its tether it broke.

Scared and excited, it ran amok.

A pail of milk it knocked down,

Then kept on going round and round.

The Jut was roiled; he yelled in anger.

Jut   O wife, here is another hungry[1] beggar.

Give him some food; get rid of this parasite.

In appearance he is a yogi, but not quite.

His eyes have the gleam of a cad.

I am afraid he'd do something bad.

He assails like a soldier on raid.

He makes me feel as if I'm afraid.

Narrator The yogi glared at him long and hard,

Gathered a deep frown on his forehead.

His bowl on one hand he balanced.

A Jut by a yogi was challenged.

———————————————

The Jutti rose; she was determined

To make up for the milk that was spilled.

She scratched his face, his clothes she tattered;

Ranjha and all his ancestors she cursed.

Unspeakable speech she freely used—

Spat out words fiery and lewd,

Which roused the yogi to such a degree

He forgot decorum and propriety.

Wildly he swung, hit her on the mouth.

Two of her front teeth were knocked out.

She fell to the ground like a log of wood.

Surprised at himself, motionless the Yogi stood.

Narrator Alarmed, the Jut raised a hue and a cry.

Jut An uncouth bear has struck a fairy.

This vagabond yogi has killed my spouse.

He did this to me in my own house!

O my friends, come to my aid;

A mess of my world this rascal has made.

He crept in from behind like a demon.

Here is an evil man if ever there was one.

Narrator The call for help many villagers heard.

Together they came, roused like a herd.

Pikes and clubs the young men carried.

No one in the village tarried.

The yogi thought it prudent to find a way

Of quickly and stealthily getting away.

Women came and made much fuss,

Learned the truth and were furious.

Woman A fakir has killed a woman.

Someone call the king's guardsmen.

Narrator   The yogi lost his composure, scurried
 about

Until he managed to sneak his way out.

He was proud he tricked everyone.

None of them knew where he had gone.

There was a lesson for the village women.

A yogi very well might be a charlatan.

The yogi restarted his interrupted begging.

With food soon his bowl was filling.

Alms some gave him smilingly.

Others abused him verbally.

Some chastised him harshly.

He found the Kheras' house by and by.

25. Khera Residence

---

1 The bed was often used by women to sit on.
They sat cross legged.

Ranjha   Who owns this huge mansion?

I see only a mean looking woman.

Where are the elders, who might have a good head?

A young girl I see sitting on a bed.[1]

Sehti *(to Heer)* O Sister, yogi the rascal is here.

Freshly pierced are both his ears.

(He had pierced his ears for this occasion.)

He is no yogi, but someone perverse.

 I am afraid he brings us a curse.

Narrator Eager to enter, the yogi came running

Like a hawk after its prey swooping.

Like a soldier he came charging,

Looking forward to a battle winning.

Rashly, the Kheras' yard he entered.

Loudly his conch he tooted.

Then softly he whispered sarcastically

Ranjha   Hello, Khera's wife, you look happy.

Sehti   Tell me the truth, O fake Yogi.

Why do you like harassing me?

In the king's garden you lope blithely.

(We allow you freedom in our beautiful country.

You are taking advantage of it.)

Ranjha   You certainly are a quarrelsome lass.

You wear earrings and a golden necklace.

For what reason so well dressed are you?

(Something is afoot; what are you up to?)

Like a peacock you are pretty.

Why do you choose to quarrel with a yogi?

Sehti You are the one who maligned me yesterday.

Like a demon you come pursuing me today.

Ranjha You are young and too passionate.

Misleading and false accusations you create.

Spit out whatever you have to say.

You don't realize you act in a crude way.

Sehti   Come good people, come and see

This crook and swindler of a yogi.

How he lies so blatantly!

26. Ranjha and Sehti Skirmish

Ranjha   Why do you our progress hamper?

Sehti They talk of you everywhere,

And wonder how low you are.

You would see the light only when

With heavy clubs you are beaten.

Narrator The neighbor woman, older and wiser,

Approaching Sehti, said in an admonishing manner:

Neighbor Are you crazy, you reckless daughter?

Quarreling with a yogi is not kosher.

Yogis are innocent; they know no vice.

They eat what they beg, live on bread and rice.

No home they have; to our land they are alien.

They trust only God, pin their hopes on the One.

All night they meditate on God's name.

They are honest and candid, play no game.

Sehti *(to Ranjha)* You act like a man in love—
you sigh too often.

You are no disciple of a guru genuine.

Ranjha No one is as merciful as Merciful God,
None as callous as Nemrod.

No one here is as candid as we are.

No one so stubborn as you are.

Sehti   Go on carping.

I am listening.

Ranjha Some people don't deserve to walk
   on this earth.

They do no good to home and hearth.

There are certain duties that everyone must accept.

There are certain ways that everyone must act.

A man who reneges his word is contemptible.

A warrior who eschews battle is detestable.

A matron who neglects her house is culpable.

A stubborn woman makes her family miserable.

A fakir accepts pain; a fool avoids suffering.

God loves you, even if you're worth nothing.

Sehti   You are so wise!

What a pleasant surprise!

Ranjha   All good deeds only men do—women
 don't do their share.

They eat food that is not kosher, are dirty like a leper.[1]

Sehti   A yogi you'd never be, no matter how
 long your hair grows;

No matter how much you pretend, your
 shamelessness shows.

You walk erect, your mustache hangs low.

Yoga has its secrets, that fake yogis don't know.

Ranjha   We fear you not; your threats are all useless.

Your accusations too are completely powerless.

Sehti   Your holy necklace may be precious.

It produces no respect among us.

We'd drive you out; you'd be in despair,

As the devil is when driven out by holy prayer.

Ranjha   Some are connoisseurs of hashish,
 others of sherbet.

We judge a person by his character.

A good turn leads to a good re-turn, an ill turn

---

[1] These words of Ranjha do not represent the
 prevailing cultural attitude toward women.
 Ranjha is using these words to make Sehti angry.

drives you lower.

Sehti We women are not dumb; magicians
 we can best.

Many gurus have we laid low. Listen to us, lest

You go the same way as your predecessors.

Ranjha You seek to be our equal, what is your
qualification?

Men are learned; we never see such a woman.

Sehti A woman is selfless; she never hurts anyone.

Get lost, you fake, or your days are done.

Ranjha No pain or sorrow he would suffer

Whom we show our special favor.

Your sister-in-law would soon be well,

Were we to ever treat her.

Sehti Who taught you medicine?

Was it Aristoo or Lukman?[1]

Ranjha We are like a black serpent; we've sanctity.

If you talk ill of us, you invite a catastrophe.

Many specialized charms we have created.

One cleanses the house that's hate infested.

Another reunites the lovers separated.

Yet another finds the mate for the un-mated.

From your home we'll eradicate all woe.

---

[1] Plato or Aristotle

It's no choice of ours: God has decreed so.

Narrator Heer noticed that the yogi claimed

That he could reunite the lovers estranged.

Heer Dear yogi, you speak an unwitting lie.

Who can bring back the friends who have gone by?[1]

I've looked all over, but none have I found

Who such a miracle has ever performed.

I'd give my skin to make his shoes

Who the agony of my broken heart soothes.

He is the raiment of my soul,

Who the broken heart can make whole.

What is lost to fate we can't recoup.

Why seek solace in false hope?

A Jut sees his fields burned to the ground.

How is he going to dress his wound?

If an eagle loses to a lowly crow,

What transformation does its pride undergo?

Meaning No human can unite the soul and the body

And bring love to its fruition.

It requires the ability to comfort and soothe,

But few possess this magical salve.

Narrator Sehti changed her tone.

---

[1] The words "those who have gone" are so used that
   they also mean "those who have died," so that their
   return is not possible.

She had a covert reason.

Sehti You fakirs are His favorites; He guides
 what you do.

My sister-in-law is sick; we don't know what to do.

She looks downcast; daily she is getting weaker.

Although her speech is sweet, polite is her demeanor.

She is our treasure; the situation is difficult.

She hates her husband as pagans hate the Prophet.

Her illness causes us worries terrible.

We indulge her as much as possible.

I beg you to take a look at her—please be so kind.

If you start with her hand, I'm sure she won't mind.[2]

Ranjha With checking her pulse, we should start.

Tell us the history—what's in her heart?

How is her taste? Has she lost appetite any?

Does she ever cry? Does she find anything funny?

All kinds of diseases we can cure, but the
 method must be proper.

Before we make a judgment, we must examine her.

Sehti Many doctors came, did their examination;

Nothing they accomplished—only deterioration.

Something in her is broken,

------

[2]   Out of modesty, many women did not allow male
       doctors to examine any part of their body
    except the hand.

And what's broken cannot be unbroken.

What's written in this case

No wise man can erase.

Ranjha God shows his will through a fakir's
  decision.

What the fakir advises, to it you should listen.

The body heals if God so wills;

God's acts through the Yogi's skills.

As the first step, let us see the patient.

Only then would we diagnose the ailment.

Sehti Let it be, O yogi; all your tricks are a waste.

You have cheated many others, but not the Jut caste.

We Juts are a very different breed.

In swindling us you would never succeed.

Ranjha Speak softly; why raise your voice?

The Providence feeds all; it's not your choice.

It comes from God, but cure lies with us

Because of the occult knowledge that we possess.

If you don't let me treat your sister,

Needlessly she would continue to suffer.

She would remain confined to her bed.

Let me examine her; use your head.

Sehti What kind of doctoring do you vend?

Watch out, your chicanery is about to end.

Ranjha God has sent you a trustworthy physician.

It'd be difficult to find another one.

Sehti   You dressed yourself up with ashes.

That does not deceive us leave these premises.

Ranjha Her husband is an owl; she is a bird pretty.

A victim of gross injustice is she.

Doesn't she deserves your sympathy?

Heer*(to herself)* He calls my husband an owl,
 me a bird pretty.

I think he truly sympathizes with me.

Is he, by any chance, my own Ranjhan?

I should take a look and get it over and done.

However, I must be careful of Sehti.

I don't want her to see

My reaction, if the yogi is indeed Ranjhan.

Narrator Sehti insisted that because of modesty
Heer must remain veiled fully.

Heer *(wearing a veil)* Come, dear friend,
 don't mislead me.

Why should a person smile, if he is not happy?

Why share with alien stranger yogis

What the secret of one's heart is?

Even if I did trust you,

There is no hope, so why so much ado?

Ranjha So long as lasts the celestial firmament,
Live and creative is the human ferment.

We have performed a divination,
And have obtained this information:
He was young, so was she;
They fell in love instantly.
He with his flute, she with her eyes
Won each other's heart likewise.
He sold himself in love's marketplace,
Accepted cow herding for her sake.
Happy he was 'till she got wedded.
Speedily downhill his life headed.
He pierced his ears, joined the yogis.
Then he showed up at her premises.
Narrator Alerted by what she heard, Heer sat upright.
Heer *(to herself)* All the clues seem to be just right.
 This yogi is like the one I expected.
His speech is to the point, very well-articulated.
He speaks of the flute accurately.
The story of cow-herding is also orderly.
Heer *(addressing Ranjha)* O Yogi, tell me,
   which way did that thief go
And left her wallowing in her lonely sorrow?
Why did he heartlessly pass her by?
She must now wish she would rather die.
Ranjha Our divination tells this: he has not gone far.
He is still around; something he is looking for.

Narrator   Heer laughed softly, then whispered.

Heer   Sehti might hear, watch your word.

Ranjha   An intelligent person need not be told.
A faithful friend need not be watched.

Narrator   Sehti again objected that because of modesty
Heer was not allowed to show her face fully.

Ranjha   This custom of purdah[1] is harmful.
It hides the beauty of the beautiful,
Makes the life of lovers difficult.
Unnecessarily it causes them hurt.
Discard your veil, so that we might see
Your face as well as your eyes.

Sehti (to Heer) He has got you under his spell.
I'm afraid that doesn't bode very well.
I see you two are colluding.
 Don't you see how he is conniving?

Ranjha   We are alone; you two are united.
You are both pretty, but your scheming is blighted.
Let's not prolong this meaningless spat.
Give us some food, and leave it at that.

Narrator   Ranjha had heard a rumor
That Sehti had a clandestine lover,
Who rode a camel in the desert.

-----

[1] Segregation of women, and keeping them veiled.

Ranjha (to Sehti) On a young man your eyes
are set
Who rides a camel in the desert.

Sehti   What of camels? Your accusation is fiendish.
Why do you my ruination wish?

Ranjha You two are united in maligning us
One yelps as the other mocks us.
No manners you have of any sort.
Of your company I want no part.

Sehti (to herserlf) O God, what a mess I am in!
Entangled with a man who is so mean.
He should be put to hard labor
To divert him from his evil endeavor.

(to Heer) O sister, these yogis have long tentacles.
Never should you buy what a yogi sells.
If you heed them you won't do very well.
In keeping you tangled they all excel.

Ranjha You Juttis are known to be good matrons.
You take care of your husbands and sons.
Why are you hostile to this poor fakir?
Is it anger, or some kind of fear?

Sehti   If I could only lay my hands on you
You'd learn what's false, what's true.

Heer (to Sehti) Why do you harass this poor yogi?
He is harmless; listen to me:

It's a sin to hurt God's people.

It's our duty to take care of them well.

In this lies your own welfare,

That you give them a little tender care.

If you make a fakir angry,

A catastrophe might visit your country.

Sehti   It's difficult to deal with this rascal yogi.

The difficulty is greater when you oppose me.

These yogis deserve no special reverence.

They too roam seeking sustenance.

All this yoga is just a pretense.

Heer   No, Sehti, your words you will repent.

Don't forget they're like a black serpent.

Sehti   You take his side, which handcuffs me.

He is a rogue, deserves no mercy.

Heer   I am sorry you speak ill of the yogi.

Your own demise your ill would be.

Sehti   If he is stubborn

I too stand firm.

Heer   If you continue to struggle with him

You hurt yourself, not him.

Sehhti   Sister, what is this hostility

That you have lately developed for me?

You treated me like this never before.

You make me worry 'bout you more and more.

Heer   The moral order of the day has decayed.

With false accusations a chaste daughter is paid.

Sehti The yogi has created a gulf between us,

 for which I don't blame you.

With a mantra or a potion he has changed you.

(to her maid, Rabil) Get up, Rabil, and give him

  something to eat

A cupful of flour, but no meat.

I don't want to go on fighting anymore.

Push him out and lock the door.

Narrator Rabil brought a handful of millet grain,

 put it in the yogi's bowl.

Rabil   Here yogi, here is a little dole.

Narrator First she nudged him seductively,

Then blocked his way invitingly,

Stroked his face romantically.

Suddenly she called for help, screaming loudly.

When Rabil and Sehti treated him in this manner

Ranjha was roiled, lost his temper.

Ranjha This food is good enough only for a bird.

This is an insult that must be redressed.

It's mean to give a yogi only millet grain,

As only meat to a Brahman.

Sehti   Your show of anger is hypocrisy.

It does not at all impress me.

Your show of pride is also spurious.

Get you going; don't tangle with us.

Narrator Ranjha seethed with red hot anger,

Paced the yard like a caged tiger.

Ranjha You foolish woman; you she-cur.

Take this millet back to your mistress.

Sehti *(to Rabil)* Why did you not give him some alms?

He is a low person, means to do us harm.

Rabil Why did you send me to a person so hated?

My body he insulted; my modesty he violated.

Why do you push me toward my demise?

Go and find out if he treats you otherwise.

Ranjha This matter can't end in a peaceful disposition.

Too far has taken us your opposition.

We're left with no choice but to battle,

Although fighting is against our principle.

Heer I am your devotee, sir; your help I need.

I have lost my parents; a new home I need.

I am an alien in this country—nothing of my
love remains.

No happiness I have; all I have is pain.

Narrator Heer admitted that with her in-laws
she was not happy,

Which disgusted and inflamed Sehti.

Sehhti You whore, beloved of a lowly servant.

You sit like a bride, looking innocent.

Your eyes encourage new lovers, although

 indifference you feign.

You seduce boys and men, but make me the villain.

Narrator   Frustrated, Sehti gave Ranjha some food.

Ranjha   This food is no good.

Sehti   It's time we called our militia out.

Nothing less would control this lout.

Narrator Ranja was so angered he dropped his bowl,

Shattered the vessel, spilled the dole.

Ranjha   When you give, give intelligently.

The act of charity must me kindly.

Sehti   Watch yourself; mind what you say.

No bad word I have said; let's keep it that way.

Ranjha   If your secret you wish me to keep,

 Why did you cause my bowl to break?

 If innocent is your affair,

Why do you keep it hidden from your mother?

Of a clandestine affair you accuse your sister.

Are you doing any better?

Sehti   My protector saint would speak for me

When God in the next world questions me.

Heer   You are unfair and whimsical.

You broke his bowl, then rake him on coals.

Sehti Sister, your sanctimony is the same as ever.

You preach at me while looking for another
lover.

You think he is a saint, wiser than the wise.

I know he is a charlatan in a yogi's guise.

Heer   Don't insult the holy yogi.

You are asking for trouble surely.

Sehti   I would kill him, or myself slay.

There is left no other way.

Heer   You are so excited.

If you could, you'd see me executed.

27. Ranjha and Sehti Fight

Narrator Sehti and Rabil for a weapon looked around;

Two wooden clubs soon they found.

They rushed at him, knocked him to the ground;

Gave him a thrashing utterly sound.

Narrator   So insulted, Ranjha lost his temper.

Two frail fairies now faced a big bear.

Wildly he attacked the weaker women.

He was hot like an underground oven.

He underestimated his adversary,

Who had a much larger army.

A few strong women came rushing in.

Like a pack of hounds, they zeroed in.

The high soaring falcon now lay on the floor.

They shut up Heer, locked the door.

Ranjha could do nothing anymore.

The women pushed him out the door.

Ranjha landed on a pile of dirt;

Never had his pride been so hurt.

Ranjha *(musing)*   Heer is muted. I lie in dirt.

I've lost my chance; no hope is now left.

I've lost my woman; my pride also.

A joke I would be wherever I go.

I sought love, found millet grain;

Got beat up in the bargain.

O God, you are inexorable.

You gave me a fate terrible.

My ship had arrived; why did it back roll?

Why did you bring me so near my goal?

Why did you bless then damn me?

Were my sins so bad you couldn't forgive me?

Narrator Ranjha received a message from above

In a sweet voice full of love.

Voice   Since the five saints support you,

Nothing should ever discourage you.

If you show firm resolve

All your difficulties would be solved.

Narrator Ranjha then came to remember

Balnath was his spiritual father.

Narrator Knowing that the five saints were on his side,

Ranjha was encouraged, started to fantasize.

Ranjha (fantasizing) With black magic I'd
  ravage their land,

Torch all their fields, leave them only sand.

I'd tie up Sehti, the whore-bitch-witch,

Toss her over into a deep ditch.

My black tongue would lick all my enemies.

I'd bring Heer back from across the seven seas.

I'd assail my foes from every side.

They would find no place to hide.

28. Ranjha Moves to Black Land

Narrator Lost in thought, worried deeply,

Ashes smeared all over his body,

Ranjha thought the matter over—

Cogitated, but found no answer.

He resolved to leave the Khera land

And migrate to the barren Black Land.

He established himself under a large tree,

Raised an enclosure to mark his territory.

Everyone's forgiveness he obsequiously begged,

Closed his eyes and sat cross legged.

Ranjha I was wrong; now I pray,

Please, dear God, show me the right way.

Narrator   He spun a web of deception.

Ranjha Love and musk cannot be hidden.

(My innocence is self-evident.)

Narrator   No doubt his anguish was real,

For losing Heer was a true ordeal.

His eyes closed, he prayed earnestly.

Deep was his sorrow; he cried continuously.

He thought of nothing but God and His mercy.

He prayed every way—secretly and openly,

Wore ashes like a yogi, danced like a Sufi.

Like pagans, butter on coals he sprayed.[1]

Both to Allah and Bhagwan[2] he prayed.

To strengthen his will, he employed deep breathing.

Gained deep trances by assiduously meditating.

A mark he developed on his forehead.

A mysterious voice suddenly he heard.

Voice   Tomorrow is the day when the battle

comes to a head.

29. New Messenger

---

[1] A pagan ritual used to create holiness.

[2] Hindu supreme god.

Narrator   A group of girls went for a walk.

Like a flock of birds they landed in a park.

They saw the abode of a new yogi,

And headed toward it eagerly.

They put out his lamp, broke his bowl.

His precious opium in dust they rolled.

His plates and cups they mischievously shattered.

Fruits and vegetables all over scattered.

They even knocked over his box of holy ashes,

And spilled his precious hashish caches.

The yogi couldn't maintain his dignity.

Ridiculous he looked in his near-nudity.

It was a sudden ambush; the yogi was helpless.

The girls left behind quite a big mess.

Stealthily they retreated, having had their fun.

All of them escaped, but for one.

Ranjha *(roaring)* Ha! I got you; you are
     my prisoner.

You will pay for your misbehavior.

Narrator   He beat his hand-drum and
     loudly roared.

His eyes were glowing eerily red.

This scared the poor girl to such an extent

She broke out in a loud lament.

Girl   Please, sir, don't hit me.

If you hit me, I might die.

You're a giant; I'm a fairy.

Please forgive me; I beg mercy.

Perhaps I can be of some use to you.

A message I'd gladly deliver for you.

Meaning   Just in time the help came from above.

 Ranjha found a messenger of love.

Narrator   The Girl kept her word, acted as a messenger.

 Faithfully she delivered each and every letter.

Ranjha's Letter   You thought you acted prudently,

My world you ravaged consequently.

The earthquake you wrought was a violent one.

You shook my world to its foundation.

I was drowning, pitiful was my plight.

You didn't rescue me, 'though I was in your sight.

The fire of grief drove me mad.

A horrible time of it I had.

You ruined my life violently

As Mongols do their enemy.

Next you married my adversary.

Cavalierly you then abandoned me.

I followed you to your newly established house.

Like a thief I was beaten; I retreated like a

 mouse.

Narrator Having delivered the letter,

A few words the messenger had to offer.

Messenger Girl Discouraged, he now lives in
 the Black Land.

You can't with clear conscience let go of his hand.

Such is the code of love—as you must know.

You broke the code; you fell low.

People talk of you contemptuously.

They judge your conduct cowardly.

Your soul left you, went her own way.

All that was left was a statue of clay.

Among your in-laws you lived like a queen.

How much you hurt him you've never seen.

To live like a yogi now he aspires.

His goal now is to curb his desires.

In God's hands he has left everything,

Stoically accepts what fate might bring.

You forsook poor Ranjha.

Made a life with a Khera.

If such a devious intent you had,

With grief why did you drive him mad?

For you he would readily give his life.

It's mean if you add to his strife.

Your youth has only a little time to go.

It lasts as long as a cloud's shadow.

You mustn't hurt a devoted lover

Even if it imperils your own welfare.

It's not right for you to procrastinate

Go to him; mind, you are not late.

Narrator Heer approached Sehti, seeking a favor.

Heer Forgive my mistakes; it is human to err.

Dear sister, I come to ask a favor.

Sehti I seek nothing from others, only their
  goodwill.

If someone insults me, I keep my counsel.

Amity is enough to keep me happy.

In conflict with others I don't like to be.

Anger taints the purity of the soul.

I try my best to keep it under control.

Heer Forgive me if I said anything unpleasant.

I beg you humbly, please pay attention.

Share my pain like a good sister.

I would be grateful to you forever.

A compatriot is visiting me.

An old and a trusted friend is he.

He had the status of a Chaudhary,

Which he renounced to make me happy.

Sehti The Satan is accursed; the Heaven he
  won't enter.

Nor would the liar, nor the usurer.

(You too are a sinner, you opposed me.

You should not expect to be forgiven.)

My heart is cleansed of every ill emotion

I refuse to foment any alienation.

I was manhandled by a yogi.

What greater insult can there be?

Meaning Sehti is hypocrisy incarnated.

Heer   It is obligatory among all humans

To share each other's pains and burdens.

We are enjoined to spread no poison,

But help even strangers and aliens.

I beseech you, like a good sister,

Help me in my time of danger.

Let's visit the yogi; make amends.

Do as the holy man recommends.

Narrator   Sehti had a change of heart—

No doubt a covert agenda she had.

Narrator   Sehti prepared a tray full of sweets,

To which she added one gold piece.

This offering to the yogi she presented,

Who turned away, as if offended.

Ranjha We seek the straight, righteous way.

You drive us toward the Hell's gateway.

A woman was the cause why Adam

Was expelled from the garden of Eden.

Deception is part of the nature of women.

They reduce rich rajahs to poverty.

Warriors they change into docile yogis.

Sehti The belly is the cause of moral
  degradation, not women.

Bread led man to lose Eden.[1]

The Satan is certainly masculine.

A bad name women are undeservedly given.

Adam caused Eve enormous trouble,

But to him she remained faithful.

Men like futile war and battle.

They are the source of the most of trouble.

It's men who are thieves and robbers.

It's men who side with wrong-doers.

Meaning *Womankind is pleasing.*

She is God's greatest blessing.

Ranjha How many times have women
  betrayed men?

Numerous are their deficiencies,

Which only a fool fails to see.

Sehti Women are the guardians of home and hearth.

---

[1] According to one Muslim interpretation of the
Genesis, Adam had to leave Eden because he ate
wheat, and from then on had to earn his livelihood.

They give meaning to birth and death.

Ranjha   Face the truth: it is obvious

All your claims are spurious.

Sehti   It is the male pride that's false; women

they condemn—

Treat them as if they were nothing but scum.

Who gave you birth, a man or a woman?

But for women human race would end.

Don't forget, many came before you.

No doubt they were far mightier than you:

Nimrod, Pharaoh, and Alexander;

Generals, kings, knights, and others.

Pride has never served anyone,

But to this vice men still hang on.

Ranjha   We know all your shenanigans.

Tell me, how many webs have you spun?

Sehti   If you are so clever, answer this:

I brought an offering; tell me what it is.

I brought a tray; covered it remains.

Tell me, wise man, what it contains.

How much cash did I add to the gift?

Can you tell me without looking at it?

Meaning *Can you tell what's in my heat?*

Ranjha   To require a yogi to perform a miracle

Is to doubt him—it is not acceptable.

God's wrath it might unleash,

But if you insist, I comply with your wish.

You have rice and sugar in the tray;

Over it a gold piece for ostentatious display.

Meaning In your heart I see only greed.

Sehti You are one of the professional cheaters,

But we are not afraid of tricksters.

Ranjha Look within your heart; it's full of doubt.

Uncover the tray; you might find out

What your doubting is all about.

Narrator Sehti took her time, uncovered the tray
 gingerly.

The rice and sugar were still there, but there was
 no money!¹

The miracle destroyed her faithlessness.

She who had challenged his piousness

Now doubted her observation—

Admitted that she had been mistaken.

She changed her mind; assumed a posture respectful.

Meaning The disappearance of the money implies

---

¹ Sehti's uncovering the tray is a metaphor for
exposing her superficial feeling. Since the money is
for *ostentatious display,* its disappearance means
that Sehti's heart is purified. Ranjha does not play
a trick. The money disappears because Sehti's
perception changes.

Sehti's has become less greedy.

Ranjha   Like a she-serpent you reign in your den,
But your pride has no justification.
You engaged in a battle with a holy man.
What's worse, you brought in other women.
Along with your maid you cursed me,
With wooden clubs you thrashed me.
Now you see the powers of a yogi
And yelp like an orphaned puppy.

Sehti   My sins were unwitting; I am fallible,
But of reforming I am capable.
Adam erred, was expelled from Eden.
Pharaoh erred, drowned in an ocean.
If I keep erring,
I'd end up in the Hell burning.

Ranjha All your life you rode a high horse,
Now you're humbled for better or worse.
The house of your delusions won't stay erect,
For its foundation has a serious defect.
You tormented a meek yogi.
He was patient, bore it stoically.
Now you've learned through experience
How powerful is the holy silence.
If you have faith in God's mercy
He arranges your affairs favorably.

I beg you, you arrogant girl, leave me alone.

I hold no malice: I forgive what you've done.

I only ask you this little favor:

Bring your sister-in-law to see me here.

Sehti   Your order I will gladly obey.

I know now I was going the wrong way.

You performed a true miracle,

Saved me from a spiritual debacle.

Ranjha *(musing)*   Dear Heer, let me see you

 for a moment.

None of my other desires is so ardent.

My days are a stretch of gloomy distress.

My nights are a spate of miserable darkness

Be kind to your servant of old.

I hope I'm still in your memory's hold.

Sehti   I am now devoted to you.

I promise I will bring to you

Your charming and beautiful beloved.

To me your words are truly sacred.

I beg you this, O dear yogi:

Kindly arrange for me to see

The one whom I love passionately.

Change his fate so he comes to me.

Narrator   Sehti went home, sat down with Heer,

And whispered confidentially in her ear.

Sehti   The beggar we drove away yesterday,

As a noble yogi he returns today.

I think you would make him very happy

If you pay him a visit shortly.

He now has the knowledge of the occult.

Much has he improved his mind and spirit.

You should do this expeditiously,

Ask for his forgiveness personally.

I think you owe him a decent offering.

A storm is looming in the offing.

Every moment it's growing stronger.

If you manage to gain his favor

You might avert the coming disaster.

Heer   To see him I will certainly go.

This lucky opportunity I will not let go.

Narrator Heer trotted along so ebulliently

She was dancing inadvertently.

She unveiled herself partially

To arouse his passion teasingly.

Ranjha saw Heer for only a moment,

Was so dazed he lost all judgment.

He felt confused; his mind wandered,

His body shook, his heart fluttered.

His thinking lost its clarity.

He blurted out haphazardly:

Ranjha *(musing)* The weather is fair,
  flowers are blooming,
Darkness is gone, the sun is shining.
I think that our luck is turning.
A new chaste life is in the offing.
Heer   I swear, I remain blameless
(I did not share my husband's bed.)
I call upon God to be my witness.
Ranjha You would be mine—your
  parents so promised.
It was not your fault if later they reneged.
(If you made any mistake, it was not your fault.)
Heer   We pay for our errors: Noah's own daughters
Drowned, because they didn't mind their father.
And Jacob's sons were cruel to their brother.
In the end they were the losers.
Abel and Cain unadvisedly fought;
A tragic result in the end they wrought.
I too erred; my parents I trusted.
Oh! How treacherously I was jilted!
They drugged me, then bound me
And sent me away—what perfidy!
Had I predicted their deception,
I would've run away to another jurisdiction
Where I could have chosen freely.

Alas! Their deception I did not see.

Ranjha A match for you your parents located,

I was left alone, devastated.

I thought the marriage made you happy:

I thought you had betrayed me,

Which is the reason why I was angry.

Heer Every human tastes something of pain.

Everyone has a reason to complain.

Like a beehive, life offers honey.

It also stings like a wild bee.

Love is a rose, but ironically

Its thorns do not know mercy.

If you don't mind, I would like to go home.

With Sehti's help, I plan to escape from

The house that tyrannically imprisons me.

How, dear Ranjhan, I want to be free!

Narrator Heer went home where she

talked to Sehti.

Heer Dear Sehti, we should make a plan.

Escape from here as soon as we can.

For my sake Ranjha suffered a lot.

It is my duty to do my part.

You want with Murad to unite;

To me, then, it seems quite right

The two of us should make a team.

Together we should develop a scheme.

You want to live your life with Murad, I with Ranjhan.

Let's cooperate—unite the two goals in one.

Narrator Other girls in Khera's household

Made fun of Heer, for their hearts were cold.

Girls Tell us, sis, what brightens your mien?

Have you beguiled another someone?

Like a golden bird you are brilliant.

Like a bunny you are ebullient.

You looked half-dead, and all of a sudden

You are alert like a thief on the run.

Tell us what your secret might be.

We've never seen you so happy.

Is your youth in its second bloom?

Is there someone in the forest whom

With your wiles you have vanquished?

The lamp of his holiness lies extinguished.

Your cheeks are red, as is your abdomen

You have been lying by the side of someone.

You've been playing a real fast one.

You have been to see your Ranjhan.

Heer It's the heat that makes my face red.

With vexation I cried, so my eyes are red.

A calf I tried to rein in.

It rubbed against my abdomen.

Girls   To hoodwink us do not even try.

Certainly, you are doing something sly.

Heer My days of youth I have forgotten,

But it seems as if someone

Is stirring up old memories.

I think an impostor this yogi is.

Girls   Oh dear, how very sad!

Is your lover really so bad?

Heer   O sisters, it doesn't become sisters

To make fun of their unfortunate sister.

Girls Certainly, someone has been quite callous.

A good for nothing your lover is.

Heer   My dear sisters accuse me falsely.

I am distraught; what hope is there for me?

Girls Come, we know what you are up to.

You think we don't see the real you?

Heer   I'm innocent, please believe me;

I know no tricks, nor hypocrisy.

Girls   All right, the truth we do not know.

You take your turn, you tell it now.

What should we make of the mien of guilt

When you came back from your visit?

Heer   I was going along in the town

When, all of a sudden, I was knocked down

By a spooked, loosened bull

Which has made me look so frightful.

Girls   Oh yes, for sure.

The bull has been after you forever.

Heer   Alas! With poor luck I was born.

I sought a flower, found a thorn.

Girls   You had been looking haggard.

You won't blame us if we wonder

Why, suddenly, you look so pretty.

What the cause of this miracle might be?

30. The Plan to Escape

Heer*(musing)* A long time lasted the blighted drought.

Then the rain came; flowers it brought.

The grass greened; the vines rose aloft.

Narrator Sehti and Heer agreed tacitly

To mislead the girls deliberately.

Sehti spoke out quite loudly:

Sehti   She tells lies shamelessly.

A web of deception she consummately weaves.

God and the Quran she never heeds.

Narrator   Sehti visited her mother, told her

The most brazen lies you've heard ever.

Sehti *(to her mother)* We thought we had

 found a bride pretty.

As luck would have, a jade was she.

For right and wrong she has no mind.

To her husband she is never kind.

She has been recalcitrant from the first day—

Won't agree with you, no matter what you say.

She prefers solitude, claims to be ill,

Never acknowledges our goodwill.

A daughter-in-law should her in-law's house
    brighten.

With her melancholy everything she darkens.

Mother   An elephant is the pride of an army.

It is kosher for a person with money

To eat and dress well without remorse.

A man may take pride in his horse.

Such are the well-known nature's laws

A daughter-in-law adorns the house of her in-laws.

(This is one of the important social laws.)

To wish him ill who wishes you well

Does not behoove decent people.

(We should not fault Heer, for she means well.)

To this advice all daughters should listen:

Women should sincerely love their men.

Sehti   She never socializes with any of us.

She acts like she is better than us.

She does not like our people or village.

Our noble name she has damaged.

No good she does us, 'though she is pretty;

We cannot sell or eat her beauty.

The mullah, the soothsayer, the medicine man

All cost money; how long we can

Afford to pay tribute to our queen?

A woman so spoiled I have never seen.

She should be locked up in a room with her husband.

Let Saida settle his score with her—and

Let her cry, wail, and raise rumpus

Even if it bring ill name to us.

I don't care; I am tired of her hubris.

Narrator Sehti was sure that these words of hers

Had convinced her naïve mother

That she was no friend of Heer,

So her mother could trust her

To keep an eye on her sister.

Heer(to her mother-in-law) I would

 to see the fields, mother.

I will take Sehti along.

I have been sitting indoors too long.

---

[1] It is said that the Caliph Omar had a very clever
friend, who helped him get out of all kinds of
difficulties. He is likely a fictitious figure.

Narrator The daughters manipulated

the naïve mother.

You would think they were Omar the Clever.[1]

Mother Who stops her?

It's her own choice, she doesn't go out ever.

Sehti Perhaps we are wrong; the problem might be

It's her poor health that makes her ornery.

Your daughter-in-law might be a real gem,

That under lock and key is hidden.

She might be a rose that needs fresh air.

Some country brides are like a picture,

As delicate and fragile as Chinese paper.

They are congenial, malleable like wax,

As beautiful as Paradisiacal peacocks.

In what they do they need a free hand,

For they grow up on the open land,

Not in cities, not in purdah.[2]

Unlike city girls, they do not wear *burka*.[2]

Heer   Too much time I spend indoor.

Perhaps I should not do that anymore.

---

[2] Purda is the practice of segregating women and
keeping them veiled.

[2] Burka is the outer wear that covers a woman from
head to feet. Only women living in cities, who could
afford not to work, wore it. To a large extent, this is
true even now.

The fresh air and sunlight in the garden
I hope would help my mood to brighten.
Narrator Sehti called her friends to a meeting,
Said they needed to do some planning.
Some were single, others married.
To the meeting they all hurried.
They gathered around their ring leader
As disciples around a guru gather.
Sehti (*to her friends*) You must get up
  and come out early.
Be sure no one your exit gets to see.
Your parents must have no clue.
They must not suspect what you are up to.
Move in a group, all as one,
Then lead Heer to the garden.
Don't forget to keep encouraging her,
Then cross the field to the opposite corner.
You might be tempted to show your beauty,
But you must remain hidden thoroughly.
If you meet a passerby, you must spin fiction;
Act as if you are playing and having fun.
Look as if your spirits are high.
Make faces at every passerby.
Let no one suspect your serious mission.
Pretend that you are picking cotton.

Narrator   Sehti spent the night worrying
  and planning.

Her companions took to singing and dancing.

They seemed to have forgotten their mission.

They got occupied with having fun.

They spread the news from door to door.

Girls   Tomorrow is the battle's final hour.

The Kheras are invited also

Near the well they would meet their foe.

Narrator They busied themselves with their
  beautification:

Reddened their hands with henna coloration,

Applied to their eyes dark mascara,

Colored their lips red with *dandasa*.

Baring their bosom partially.

They displayed their beauty brazenly.

All night Sehti fervently pray'.

The next day the Inexorable had Its way.

She could do nothing to change its course;

Too great was its invisible force.

Meaning No one saw the hand of the Providence.

Nor did Sehti see the evidence.

Narrator The girls behaved terribly.

Sehti could no longer rely on secrecy.

She had to think of a new strategy.

The girls got up and started early.

They talked to their mothers openly.

In a group they walked joyously,

Their hips swinging voluptuously.

 Girl Come Sehti, what is the hesitation?

Narrator Sehti too asked her mother's permission

To go out with the girls and have some fun.

In a group they advanced as an army

Like horses on the loose, they romped freely.

31. Sehti's Plan

No one remained in the town;

They all came to see Ranjha the clown.

All kinds of games were in progress.

Sehti set to her tricky business.

She pricked Heer's foot with a long thorn,

Drew some blood, then raised an alarm:

Yelled that Heer was stung by a serpent,

And was in need of immediate treatment.

She proved her skill at venom-cure,

Sucked up the poison without any fear.

Jaws clenched, Heer held herself rigid,

Bit here lips till they were livid.

All over she shook with feverish chills,

As if haunted by a clique of devils.

Heer O dear ones, I am dying.

I am scared; please do something.

Narrator Seeing this, all the trainee devils

Left their teacher, the Master Devil,

And enrolled as Sehti's disciples.

Acting scared, Sehti made a great din.

Sehti I swear, a serpent I have seen

Sting the foot of my darling Heer.

I am going to die of fear.

Please do something to save my Heer dear.

Narrator They brought Heer home on a stretcher.

All the while she was getting ashier.

No one had ever seen or heard

Such great trickery as they now observed.

The Satan bowed respectfully—

Admitted Sehti's superiority.

Narrator To alert the town of this serious matter

The Kheras employed a drum beater.

The girls too raised a hue and cry.

Soon the emergency team came by.

The whole town heard the worrisome story.

People She sure was a bride pretty.

Her mother-in-law certainly loved her.

Her husband she would not let touch her.

It is said that she loved another.

Narrator   The Kheras employed treatments of

every kind,

Brought in every expert that they could find.

Venom-curers, fakirs, and medicine men;

Snake charmers, who played their pipes as one.

Along came also many soothsayers,

Who wrote holy names on colored papers.

Some even brought cobra milk.

Another brought a colored dice rolled in silk.

Narrator   Everyone was eager to give advice.

Older Woman   If the medicine is for one person

It does not help a different one.

If the cure is for one disease

It does not cure a different disease.

Once the poison in the body spreads

It does not avail if a mantra is said.

Second Woman   The poison has spread already.

Any moment she is likely to die.

It'd make no difference what treatment you try.

Heer   O friends I'm dying, please do something.

I sense the poison is already working.

 I feel through my liver it is running.

Sehti   No doubt we have tried everything.

Nothing at all seems to be working.

This snake won't be beaten at all

By methods that are not spiritual.

In the Black Land lives a hermit-yogi;

An accomplished curer of venoms is he.

Snakes, dragons, and two-headed ghouls

All are under his magic's rule.

He helps those who are innocent.

Kings and sages seek his consent.

Ajju (to Saida) Listen carefully, my dear son.

Cautiously you must handle this one.

Go and fetch the holy yogi.

Don't forget to touch his feet humbly.

Keep your head bowed deferentially.

Tell the venerable man the whole story.

Make sure you bring him a good offering;

Otherwise for you he would do nothing.

If at all possible, bring him with you,

No matter how much begging you have to do.

Narrator Saida put on his shoes, tightened his belt.

(These items only for travel were meant.)

He threw a shawl over his shoulder

And carried a cane like a dandy soldier.

He traveled as fast as he could.

In front of the yogi soon he stood.

Yogi *(roaring)* Who are you? Stop right there.

Speak. What is it that brings you here?

Narrator Saida was scared; in a voice meek,

With much difficulty he managed to speak,

Saida For God's sake, sir, please come with me.

I am, I swear, in great agony.

Yogi O you poor Jut, what has befallen you?

You look as if a ghost got you.

Saida She was stung by a poisonous snake.

For two days and nights I have been awake.

She was stung while picking cotton.

Come, please, precarious is her condition.

Yogi It's not wise to attempt to change fate

(And stinging by a snake is an act of fate.)

Those who love God sincerely

Are not afraid of death's finality.

Besides, the snakes (men) of the Sial country

Are above law, completely free.

Also, we've taken a vow by the Quran

Never to lay an eye on a woman.

In peace let the good Juttie die.

Certainly people would wail and cry.

Much they would mourn her demise,

Forgetting from her ashes a new one would rise.

(When the old culture dies, a new one would arise.)

Saida   O holy yogi, I beg you humbly.

Please come with me; don't let her die.

For two days straight I have been fasting.

Other venom-curers have accomplished nothing.

The Jutti was stung by a rare breed.

An especially accomplished doctor she needs.

No improvement she has shown whatsoever,

Through you, we hope, God would bless her.

O yogi, my ship is helplessly floundering.

Please pilot it; save it from sinking.

Narrator The yogi stood still for a moment then said,

Yogi We feel sorry for your predicament,

But we have our professional constraint,

Which is even true of accomplished saints.

The material world we have renounced.

In poverty contentment we have found.

I cannot change this way of living,

Although I understand your wife is dying.

I go back to the world if I go with you,

Which my vows do not allow me to do.

Besides, I should not be around women.

If I see them, it is a bad omen.

For me, seeing women is as shameful

As for a soldier to run from battle.

Saida   She cried the day I wedded her.

Since then, it has not gotten any better.

If I even come near her bed

She attacks me fiercely, as if she were possessed.

So, you see, she is still a virgin,

Although likely possessed by a demon.

Narrator   The yogi drew a circle in a corner

Stuck a knife in its center.

"Swear by God," He firmly demanded.

Saida readily did as he was bid.

Saida   I swear by God-who-is-true,

Nothing I say that is not true.

I may die of horrid leprosy

If I tell you the slightest lie.

For me, Heer is far too high.

Like the mountain peaks that touch the sky.

I am nowhere near her class.

She would never be mine, alas.

Narrator Ranjha felt that Saida hurt his honor

By claiming to be Heer's protector.

He picked up the visitor; threw him in hot ashes.

The excuse he gave was this:

Wearing dirty shoes, Saida entered his place.

He thus profaned the holy place.

He hit Saida with all his might—

With fists and feet, left and right.

Then threw him in a deep pit,

Which for human landing was unfit.

Saida ran home as fast as he could.

Soon, in front of his home he stood.

Saida   He is a fighter, not a yogi.

Wait 'till you hear my story.

He is a magician from a land alien.

Believe me, he is a really cruel one.

Like a giant he is powerful.

As of thunder, his roar is fearful.

He says his prayers, reads the Quran.

He acts like a pagan, a Hindu, and a Mussalman[1]

He beat me up mercilessly.

I bare my body, so you can see.

Ajju   Good people, this yogi is completely
   heartless.

My jewel of a son he has rendered worthless.

Other yogis come to help common folks.

This one brings us only a curse.

Sehti   Dear father, you should be the one

To fetch the yogi, not your son,

Who is arrogant, willful, and stubborn,

And doesn't think much of anyone.

---

[1]   Muslim

Narrrator Since Ajju too was very much
worried,

To fetch the holy man he expeditiously hurried.

Soon, Ajju stood before the yogi.

Ajju   God looks on you favorably.

You yogis are God's favorites.

If anyone can help me, you are it.

My daughter-in-law was stung by a snake.

My fortune I hope you can remake.

The ship of this sinner is violently reeling.

I depend on you for safe sailing.

Yogi   I have no home, no country.

You Juts still keep pestering me.

Caste or tribe I have none,

But your opposition remains stubborn.

You have been my foes from the day one.

To harass yogis is your ancient tradition.

Ajju   I ask a favor as one human to another.

Please, your blessing on us confer.

l promise you honestly that my offering

You would not find disappointing.

Narrator The yogi's body moved, his soul stirred.

He heard the singing of a happy blue bird.

The Kheras didn't wait for an auspicious day,

But came to fetch Ranjha the very next day.

They did not detect the yogi's pretense.

It was a travesty of human intelligence.

A rabbit was placed in a hawk's keeping.

A widower was assigned the job of match making.

They thought that in the yogi's person

They had found another Solomon.

Solomon turned out to be a con.

They hoped to find a new venom-curer.

He meant to set one snake against another.

In due time the Sial's were ready

To receive the new doctor-yogi.

Everyone else quietly exited.

Only the new doctor was admitted.

A girl from the Khera household mocked Heer.

Girl The Slippery Trickery Shah is here.

He plans to secretly whisk away Heer.

He spent a long time burning incense.

He'd now light a fire more intense.

The Kheras plan to give him charity.

What he would take they do not see.

God has changed his destiny.

No longer a pauper, a prince now is he.

Heer is surely uncommonly lucky.

The physician of her choice is here already.

Her pain and sorrow would be decimated,

When she by a fakir is visited.

The son of a chief who herded cows

Is a full-fledged yogi now.

To Sehti God is kind too.

She would find herself fulfilled too.

The trick is one, benefits two.

Sehti will escape along with Heer too.

Second Girl   We hear congratulations are in order.

The thirsty have found the Youth Elixir.

Conveniently was Heer stung by a serpent.

A handsome yogi will provide the treatment.

He would take her out of her hell;

To a paradise he would transfer the belle.

Certainly it was God, no creature,

Who accidentally brought them together.

Yogi   Sehti, I and Heer

 Must be left alone here—

I would be in deep meditation.

There should be no noise or motion.

 It is clearly written in the Quran:

You should punctually say your prayers.

(Go to say your prayer, so we would be alone.)

Meaning It is incumbent on every faithful

To say his prayers regularly.

Love is Ranjha's prayer.

Loving he must do constantly.

32. **Escape**

Narrator The parents asked their daughter Sehti
To stay with Heer and the yogi.
In a house in the village's periphery
They set up their abode temporary.
They put up Heer's bed in the parlor.
Ranjha was seated on the floor near her.
The parents were satisfied with this arrangement.
Their bird in the keeping of a hawk they sent.
The bride they had brought home
so lovingly
Was about to jilt them stealthily.
Sehti (to Ranjha) Please, sir, do me this favor:
God has given you great power.
Please bring my sinking ship to the shore.
I would be grateful to you forever.
All the assigned tasks I have completed.
The preparations for our escape I have completed.
The honor of the Kheras I have damaged.
My own parents I have betrayed.
I hope my services you'd keep in mind;
Let your disposition toward me be kind.

Narrator   Ranjha put himself in a praying posture,

And earnestly he said this prayer:

Ranjha (praying) She helped us out lovingly,

Saw us through our difficulty.

Please God, treat her kindly,

As in your graciousness You treated me.

Narrator The voice of the five saints came clearly.

Voice   God has decreed their union.

Sehti and Murad would soon be one.

Narrator Riding a camel, Shah Murad arrived.

Murad   Come dear, with me you ride.

My column of camels lost its way.

It seems someone has hexed me today.

Still, she-camel is the fastest around.

I'm glad that you I have found.

Narrator Heer held on to Ranjha, Sehti to Murad.

Full of hope, they proceeded westward.

A hawk saved a caged bird,

A tiger a goat from its herd.

Each couple chose its own way.

They separated after going a short way.

In the morning the whole village exploded.

In hot pursuit two pursuing parties headed.

They profaned their faith and religion;

Even women were part of the expedition.

After their beards were shaved,
The Kheras fought with their barbers.
Such is the fate of evil doers.

Some were happy over the luck of the fakir,
Others cried over the loss of Heer.
Some carried clubs, led by hate.
Others beat drums to celebrate.
When they saw Murad and Sehti,
The first pursuing party danced with glee.
Little did they know that Murad's soldiery
Had arrived during the night.
The pursuing party was put to flight.

33. Ranjha and Heer Are Apprehended

Narrator The second party pursued Heer and Ranjha,
Found them sleeping in a desolate area.
Her head on his shoulder serenely resting,
Like two innocent birds nesting.
Their swords and sabers they violently brandished.
The horsemen had them promptly surrounded.
Ranjha was helpless; he could do nothing.

They kicked him first, then took to lashing.

They kept it up unremittingly

Until they saw that copious blood was dripping.

Heer   Alas! 'cause of poor judgment

   we are ruined.

Now we are in the clutches of a fiend.

But I don't think all is lost.

We must find a solution no matter what the cost.

I suggest you might try this:

Our Rajah is fair, upholds justice.

With arms raised,[2] you might go to his court.

You get nowhere without some effort.

 Copper can yield golden money

If you have access to true alchemy.

Meaning *It the body has true faith, it must win.*

34. Ranjha at Rajah's Court

Narrator   Soon at the Rajah's court Ranjha

   appeared.

 Respectfully he pleaded to be heard.

Ranjha   May you live long, Honored Sire.

---

   [2] The legend has it that it was a custom that if a person
arrived at the king's court with arms raised, the king was
obliged to hear him.

Since God has blessed you, nothing you need
fear.

Your justice is known everywhere.

Everyone knows you are judge fair.

Other kings and sultans defer to you.

Your subjects honor and extol you.

I was abused wantonly,

'Though I did no wrong, hurt nobody.

Deviously and forcibly the Kheras robbed me

Of my most beautiful and precious possession.

No other recourse I have; to you I petition.

Please pay attention to my condition.

God will bless you for your disposition.

Narrator The Rajah's counselors started to argue

As to what the Rajah should do.

Rajah   The thieves must not get away.

If I want to catch them, arguing is not the way.

My soldiers, act! Bring the robbers to me.

My justice they would promptly see.

Narrator   The Rajah ordered, his soldier complied,

Stopped the Kheras; loudly they cried.

Soldiers Don't try any trick; let it be understood.

None of your deception would do you any good.

Come along of your own accord.

The alternative, we assure you, would be quite hard.

Narrator Before the Rajah the Kheras were
ushered

And told they would be properly heard.

His case Ranjha was asked to plead.

He was glad to take the lead.

Ranjha They stole my beloved wife from me.

They did it trickily and forcibly.

Each of them is a veteran villain.

Of their ruthlessness I complain.

I am at your mercy, O Rajah Revered.

If you judge them by their beards,

You would think they are decent men,

But their inside is like that of the Satan.

A prostitute's house is colorful outside;
  inside it is shabby.

Falsehood is all too often glittery.

Kheras We have never been unfair to anyone.

He is a great swindler, a fake herdsman.

He practices magic, can freeze oil.

As soon as he landed on our soil

He began seducing a Sial daughter.

Of seducing young women he is a master.

Our daughter-in-law was stung by a serpent.

We were desperate for good treatment.

We learned of a yogi, who in the Black Land lived.

In treating snake bites he was accomplished.

Trustingly we invited him to our house.

This is how well behaved this louse:

He abducted both Heer and Sehti!

Alas! His evil nature we did not see.

He looks like a yogi, is really a villain.

A ruler should conscientiously curb such a bane.

If you punish him, you'd do what is right:

You would cure this land of a blight.

Ranjah They saw my pretty wife and chased me—

Came up riding and surrounded me.

I feared I was in their country,

Where I was alone to fight so many.

They claim Heer is Saida's wife.

No relation of the Kheras is my wife.

Never to a Khera was married she.

They are habitual liars, they feel free

In your august court to lie brazenly.

There is no end to their trickery.

If you don't believe me, check their history.

A longer life God had granted me.

That is why they could not kill me.

They assumed her guardianship arbitrarily—

Drove me away forcibly.

Rajah I'd put them to death surely

If they robbed you of your property.

If they did anything unlawful

They would receive punishment in full.

(to Kheras) It seems it was your error.

You wronged this poor fakir. I won't let this matter rest,

Until I reach a verdict just.

These Juts, when they have some money,

Become arrogant, mind nobody.

They kill poor fakirs, abduct their women.

A web of tyranny they have woven.

They take to thieving during the night,

Abduct women in broad daylight.

Like the Satan, they harass the populace.

Certainly, the Kadi would rule against their case.

Narrator The name of the Kadi was barely
   mentioned.

Immediately he took over the interrogation.

Kadi   Tell us what the real truth is.

Like Omar Khatab, we dispense justice.

Kheras   This is the story in full:

Seeking Heer's hand was a pursuit pleasurable.

She came of a house honorable.

The Sial and Khera houses matched very well.

Many other suitors sought Heer likewise.

Saida was lucky; he won the prize.

A large wedding party we prepared.

No expense at all we spared.

Hundreds were the guests, men and women.

Hindus came as well as Muslims.

No required ritual we omitted.

Duly, the Mullah officiated.

He recited the Quran in the proper manner.

He was the witness, along with a lawyer.

All the requirements of the law we fulfilled.

A legitimate marriage the town witnessed.

Rajah How did the Kheras get stuck with Heer,

Who now wants to leave them for a fakir?

Many people warned them, did they not?

Why did they ignore such a potent caveat?

Kheras He was starving. Choochak took pity,

Took him on as a lowly employee.

Many tongues wagged, for he had a daughter.

He got worried about his honor.

When Ranjha saw the beautiful daughter,

He decided to go after her.

He got so bold he dared to aver

That he was actually engaged to her.

He claimed to be the son of a Chaudhary.

In fact, among the progeny of a drum-beater is he.

Kadi   Come, Sir Fakir, abjure your trickery.

Remember, through you we can see.

Tell us nothing but the truth.

Don't go around beating the bush.

Everyone in the town is laughing at you.

What you dished out is coming back to you.

You insulted the Juts honorable,

Not only the Sials but the Kheras as well.

You made a claim on their daughter.

We salute you; you certainly have the dare.

You have gained enough ill repute.

It's time you returned the ill-gotten loot.

Good men and women seek society.

First and foremost, a fakir seeks piety.

What Ranjha seeks in his deviousness

We all can very well guess.

Narrator Ranjha was seething with red hot anger.

He lashed out at the Kadi in this manner:

Ranjha If the house of Kheras you prefer,

Then give them, Sir Kadi, your own daughter.

Thieves feed on what others earn.

Such is the Kheras' living fashion.

If you have a point canonical,

Teach them; they would understand it well.

Kadi You crook. Give up Heer, or else

Our whip would cure your rebelliousness.

Heer goes with the Kheras, so we order.

There is no doubt this fakir is a swindler.

His heart is black like that of the Satan.

Falsely he pretends to be a holy man.

Narrator Blithely the Kheras walked away
 with Heer.

Ranjha wished he would disappear—

Dissipate in the air, never to be seen anywhere.

He hid his face, for nothing made sense.

He felt exiled from all existence.

Neither the Mother Earth nor the Father Heaven

Seemed to accept his defeated person.

He felt like he was no one.

His deeds were no longer his own.

Nothing had any meaning—all was confusion.

His world lay shattered by an invisible explosion.

Heer also stood dazed; she took off her veil.

Everything seemed quite unreal.

She saw the edge of a huge fire—

It made her wonder if it was a funeral pyre?

Was she supposed to perform *sutti?*[1]

Was she for such bravery ready?

---

[1]The Hindu custom of burning the wife along with

the body or her deceased husband.

She lost her speech, had no breath left.

Her body was alive, but of Life bereft.

Ranjha What is it that you're trying to figure out?

There is nothing left to see or sort out.

Much worse than death is this separation.

No one can know the pain or our situation.

Saida gets Heer, I get the ashes.

O God, what kind of justice is this?

Did you make this world so unfair,

The ugly crow wins the birdie fair?

Heer's lips are my Elixir of Life.

Without her I'd live without Life.

Heer The pain of separation is the worst of all pains.

In the front is fire, in the back snakes and lions.

Which way, then, should I turn?

Or am I supposed to forever mourn?

Dear God, reunite us, or end our days.

We cannot go on living this way.

Unfair has been to us this town.

May God's justice burn it down.

 I have faith; it is still possible

That we would see another miracle.

35. Heer and Ranjha Reunite

Narrator It so happened that the town caught fire.
It burned down like a dry funeral pyre.
The news soon all over the country spread.
People conjectured the fakir must have cursed.
The Rajah sent for Ranjha promptly.
He was brought to him directly.
Rajah (to Ranjha)   Dear Sir, we respect you greatly.
Take your Heer; she's yours rightfully.
No longer we doubt your piety.
We beg you, please pray for our safety.
Ranjha *(praying)* O God, You are the Light and
 Luminosity.
Please ensure this town's safety.
Let it not see another calamity.
Ensure it prospers 'till eternity.
Narrator Heer and Ranjha started on their way
to his home.
Ranjha O my dear, the mistress of my home.
You are the bride of a Hazara Chaudhary,
Thanks to the five saints' generosity.
God has brought you to a hilly country.
Heer   If I go to your country
Your people would for sure laugh at me,
Mock me that by a servant I was abducted;

My folks and in-laws I insulted.

Without proper wedding, I live in sin;

A tramp and a vagabond I have been.

Meaning   *The soul respects the rightful worldly*
traditions.

She knows this is how the world functions.

She is already married spiritually.

She admits she should be married also in a
Manner worldly.

Narrator When the hilly county they traversed

Many women came out, some of them said:

First woman   O prince of love, our hearts too

Warm up with love passionate and true.

Toward others you are generous.

Why do you selectively ignore us?

Is it because our windstorms are dangerous?

Second Woman (to Heer) You and your man
   make a strange sight.

Something there is not just quite right.

(I doubt if you are legitimately married.)

Your moon is like beauty that dispels darkness.

What kind of love has it harnessed?

Are you deluded by a romantic emotion?

Where is your intended destination?

(I fear you have no in-laws to go to.)

Is a dandy with his talk slippery,

Ruining your life, O naïve beauty?

Narrator   On the way they passed through the
  Sial ground.

Heer   Let's stop; let me take a look around.

This is the place of my happy childhood,

Where for many years I proudly stood.

Here also the Kheras' wedding party arrived.

That was the day all my happiness died.

Narrator   To Choochak, a peasant brought this news:

Peasant   Ranjha is back, and happy he is.

He owns her, and she is looking well.

He has won, though Sials are powerful.

What are you going to do about it?

Your beard he has shaved without getting it wet.

(You have been dishonored without much ado.)

Choochak   Don't let them go. I invite them—

My own daughter and her dear friend—

To be my guests for a day or two.

That's the proper thing for a father to do.

Narrator At the same time a Khera
  messenger arrived,

Seeking to take back Heer the bride.

Choochak   You Kheras have done us no good.

You perpetuated a dire falsehood.

When Heer was married, how could she
  have consented?

In effect, a dead body you carried.

Don't send us any other messenger.

 No more is open to you our door.

Narrator To stay with the Sials Ranjha was invited.

 By Heer's brothers he was transported.

 He had reservations, but came along.

They cut his hair short, 'cause it was too long,

Took off his copper rings, gave him a golden one,

And also provided him an excellent turban.

Like a guest he was seated on a divan,

Wondering all the time what was their plan.

Choochak   Let's do it the proper way

So no one has anything mean to say.

You come with a proper wedding party;

We would prepare Heer's *Doli.*[1]

Narrator Ranjha agreed naively

The hidden treachery he did not see.

36. Marriage Preparations

---

[1]Doli is the palanquin that was used to carry the bride.
 To prepare doli means to prepare for wedding.

Narrator Ranjha came home, was received
warmly.

Much deserved rest he enjoyed finally.

The news went out that Dhidu was wedding.

His tribesmen started celebrating.

Among his sisters-in-law he sat happily.

Like a brother they treated him tenderly.

Smoothly progressed the wedding preparation.

Every day was a day of celebration.

37. Heer's Death

Narrator The Sial brothers discussed the matter.

First Brother Decent people protect their honor.

Second Brother The story is known all
over the country;

We are mocked constantly.

Third Brother To receive a wound caused by a tongue
Is worse than by a snake to be stung.

Fourth Brother Even if this servant she marries,
It would not lessen our difficulties.

Fifth Brother The wound caused by a daughter's fall
No doubt is the most grievous of all.

Choochak We should poison her,

though it would a sin.

Second Brother To this desperate measure

many good men have been driven.

To kill a straying daughter, we are not the only ones.

Choochak Our other good deeds should save us.

We must rely on His mercifulness.

Narrator Heer died, the Sials buried her.

To Ranjha they sent a perfunctory letter:

Letter She died—even saints pass on.

Everything has its time, says the Quran.

We have no choice but to accept His will.

Deep in our heart we hurt still.

What God designs, must actuate.

Irrevocable is divinely prescribed fate.

38. Ranjha Dies

Narrator The messenger located where Ranjha lived.

With tears in his eyes, the letter he delivered.

Ranjha What kind of news do you have for me

That makes you cry so profusely?

Do my valuables rest safely?

Messenger It's what is most precious to you

That you have lost precipitously.

Narrator Overcome, Ranjha sighed deeply.

His breath left him permanently.

Meaning[1]   He joined Heer in another world

God had a special place for them held.

In the cause of love they remained steadfast,

Fought their *jihad* to the last.

In the world of flesh they were the losers;

In the real world, acknowledged winners.

Where there was a great celebration

Of the spiritual regeneration:

A soul loved a body, was loved back; therefore,

Returned to its home richer than before.

---

[1]   The translator has added this part.

Epilogue: Moral

*(The story of Heer and Ranjha, I believe, has a moral: it
contains a conception of how life ought to be lived. I attempt
to describe this conception here. I admit that my
interpretation is not free of flaws, and other interpretations
are possible. I offer my understanding for what it is worth.
Translator.)*

Heer and Ranjha: the soul and the body,
The celestial and the earthly,
The spiritual and the material,
The intangible and the tangible;
The eternal and the ephemeral,
The permanent and the perishable.
The body, perishable, must perish
And leave behind nothing tangible but dust:
Dust and memories intangible.
Memories alive in the clay, newly-shaped,
Fueling a new fire.
Another now moves through space.
It too leaves behind dust—
Dust and the memory of its sojourn,
The memory of the children of its devotion,
The flowers of fidelity and selflessness,
And the seeds sown,

And pain gladly owned.

The body leaves behind the essence of its deeds, their spirit.

That wanders the earth, seeks and finds another

abode of clay.

This body, this mote of dust,

It leaves behind

To guide those who've yet to come—

Footsteps etched in stone,

And Fate made malleable,

And the weight of stone lighted.

This, then, is the fate of man:

To be born, to precipitate out of existence,

As a drop out of a cloud—a cloud begotten of

the ocean.

To be shackled by the weight of the matter.

To battle the giants of iron and stone.

To suffer, to be crushed, to rise again, to prevail,

And wonder what it is all about—this battle with

the elements.

The scurrying for survival.

Is it worth it?

This, then, is the fate of man:

To ask, to seek, to find, to create

In the stony, cold, indifferent, universal silence.

The Celestial Music, the Answer

That was there before there was the Question:
To ask, seek, find, create,
In the blind expanse of darkness,
The eternally illuming beacon.
To seek, find, create
In the bosom of iron and stone
The string that vibrates, the reed that sings,
The song that celebrates and praises,
And comforts that soothe.
This song that is the panacea,
That cures all pain, brings forth the pain
incurable;
Warms the heart, also burns.
That is the salve that heals all wounds,
That inflicts the wound that has no salve,
That raises man to the heights of the Heaven,
That also crucifies.
This terrible panacea;
It sanctifies everything.
The sanctified matter glows, blooms, transforms
                                the universe,
Which sings like a bird of paradise.
This, then, is the fate of man:
To live, aware of the end of his time,
The time when the drop returns to the ocean.

To live while dying.

To live this meaningless, absurd life

With ultimate seriousness—

With the intensity of full being.

To pursue goals ephemeral, childish;

To play the game temporal,

In brief, to play with shadows

Shadows cast from beyond the horizon

Of that which remains unseen.

These shadows become carnal

And lead bodies to love.

Let bodies love, then.

Be true and faithful.

So man unites soul to soul,

And the visible and the invisible become one.

THE END

Made in the USA
San Bernardino, CA
22 January 2018